420 North

Stories from A Small Mormon Town and the Road

Alex Peterson

Crossing the Bridge, was a 2000 Brookie & D. K. Brown Fiction Contest Moonstone Winner and published in Sunstone Magazine.

ISBN: **1539038718**

ISBN-13: **978-1539038719**

DEDICATION

To my boys and my girl.

When you truly leave home you can't go back--you will return a tourist in your own town. These stories have been written over the years. Some are about living in a tiny town in Mormon country, and others are about travels. I enjoy both, but only if I can go back and forth. Too much home and I get travelsick--too much travel and I get homesick. The balance of adventure and security is never complete. Some stories are really short and some are longer. If you like to read before you go to bed, but not too much, this book could work out for you.

CONTENTS

1   420 North   Pg 1

2   The Price I Would Pay   Pg 10

3   Mud and a Hundred Dollars   Pg 12

4   Where You Are   Pg 32

5   Stouffer's Spicy Salsa   Pg 35

6   Brother Fox and the Demolition of the Devil   Pg 38

7   John John's Backpack   Pg 51

8   No Worries Man   Pg 52

9   Falling For Mila   Pg 82

10 The Big Money Wheel   Pg 86

11 The Pure Bliss of a Weed Free Yard   Pg 98

12 Crossing the Bridge   Pg 116

13 A Gay Kidney   Pg 122

420 NORTH

The whispering came to me again, this time a hint stronger than before, and my insides felt warm. It was just like what they taught me in Mormon Sunday school. The feeling was distinct—subtle, but important. I don't think it was just the sweet pork burrito talking.

I was driving back home on a lonely and long highway. The air was warm with spring and hay fever, but I had the windows down anyway after the long, dark winter. The car hit a dip at the county line, and the asphalt abruptly became more cracked and bumpy in Sanpete County. My hair blew around gently in the wind and I squinted a bit, but I refused to put on my sunglasses that lay folded on the dashboard. The dreaded dark of February was still too close to filter any bit of sunlight into my eyes and chemically challenged brain. This can't be right, I thought to myself, rejecting the promptings again.

"Get thee behind me," I whispered back. I considered rebuking the voice out loud in the name of Jesus, with my right arm to the square, with the phrase Bishop Larsen once taught me to drive away the Devil and cleanse apartments of evil spirits. But I didn't say anything. It wasn't a scary feeling. It was peaceful and calm.

"Impossible," I thought, "It just doesn't add up. This is not the way it should work."

"Try it. What have you got to lose?" The Voice whispered back. I stopped whispering and spoke aloud.

"What have I got to lose? My life in jail, for starters," I replied. "This isn't Colorado—it is Utah. Red state—not blue. Fry sauce, not

1

cannabis."

"Oh, but imagine if we could combine both states into *Utarado* or *Colorutah*. Fry sauce *and* TCH, with some fat fries for the munchies. Great idea. Uhm-hummm—brilliant. Bro, herb is natural. You can't tell me it is any worse than your list of crazy anti-depressants. Or sedatives. Or sugar. Or those huge Diet Pepsis."

"But it is obviously against the word of wisdom."

"So is too much beef."

"It is also illegal. Following the admonition of the church has kept me safe. I respect my leaders and I just can't see the brethren ever approving it."

"So what else is new? The jury is still out on coffee flavored ice cream. And you know inter-racial marriage is still a four-letter word in some households—but *Lamanite/White and Delightsome* weddings are getting more common now. Times are a changing, bro."

"It's not just the church. Pot is still not OK in a lot of America. Have you seen the Reefer Madness videos? It is a gateway drug. Even a lot of my out-of-town friends who drink think marijuana is bad."

"They say, as they pour another bottle of wine and fade into oblivion," the Voice answered sarcastically.

"My wife and kids? Hey, look, children, Dad is a pothead. Sorry, I'm just not a Spicoli type."

"Dude, you don't even have to smoke it. You can eat THC gummy bears or granola bars. You can even make it into special green Jell-O salad with shredded carrots if it makes you feel better."

"How do I know it will help? Just because Mike said it was a godsend for his depression, doesn't mean it would work for me," I replied.

"Yes. Point taken, man. It may not do anything for your mental problems. But what if it worked? What if it took the edge off or gave you back some of the sanity. What if it was actually a gift from God to you? Via Colorado?"

"Get thee behind me, Satan," I said loudly. The road was climbing up a mountain pass now, the smell of sage and earth blowing in the open windows. I rested in anticipation and thought perhaps the Voice would be gone.

"I'm still here, dude," the voice was relaxed and echoed through my head. I shifted down a gear to get the car enough torque to get over the hill.

"What kind of spirit talks like this? The Holy Lebowski?" I probed.

"Or HG, or Poltergeisterino, if you're not into the whole brevity thing. Whatever, man. You are the one talking to yourself. Plus, I don't use the F word."

The car eased over the pass and began the gradual downhill toward the mountain valley. I drove in silence. The "herbal" idea had come on gradually, with little promptings--an article here, a podcast there, a few friends from out of town. Relief from back pain, from epilepsy, from anxiety and depression. It wasn't until the past year, when I suddenly slipped and fell into a pit so deep and dark and hopeless that I nearly gave up the will to continue the trudge through life, that I took the idea seriously.

The pit drained my power and desire to move, and at the same time turned my mind into a runaway freight train on a track ending abruptly at the top of the abysmal pit of sorrow. The pit that drained my ability to experience wonder at the world and robbed my capacity for sleep. The pit that left me looking at my two beautiful boys like they were as meaningless and unfortunate as a couple of plastic Wal-Mart bags blowing through a frozen parking lot. The pit that left me wondering why the God I so desperately wanted to believe in could allow His child to feel such continuous, hopeless desolation.

Then my train wreck of a brain would remind me that things could be so much worse. I could be starving, in some terrible natural disaster in Haiti or someplace, forced to work as a shoe polisher to feed my children leftover table scraps. This cyclical shame would remind me how much more pathetic I was to feel as bad as I did while coming from a faith tradition with the Truth, living in the most blessed land of privilege on earth. The guilt and dread would pile on like gravel as I treaded water at the bottom of the pit and tried to breathe in short gasps when I could steal a breath. If God was out there he was either holding my head under water or looking the other way, busy flooding or shaking the earth somewhere. I couldn't escape. I couldn't even read. Or watch movies. Even if I wanted to talk to someone about it, my tongue was too exhausted to make words.

I tried to reach out to specialists. Most of them only had available appointments four months in advance. Eventually, I met with some. They said: try these pills, or those pills, or meditate, or count my blessings. They said sometimes you just have to keep trying the drugs until the right one works for you. It could take months or years. For someone trying to survive until tomorrow, this advice was haunting.

I forced tasteless food down my mouth to keep myself alive, with the last shred of hope that I might somehow climb out. My family was lost, struggling, and unable to help pull me up. My wife and kids screamed at me or cried next to me. The lights were not fading—they were nearly out. My pleading prayers began changing from asking for help and recovery to begging for death. I couldn't quite pull the trigger myself, but I prayed God could soon help the aneurism come or the car crash. There was no faith left, only despair.

The sounds and descriptions of a depressed person sound pitiful and trivial to someone who has merely been sad. "Just snap out of it" and "make yourself busy" sound insulting and incredibly cold to an ill mind. But if you have been in the pit, the empathy for another poor soul who is treading water below while you have found a tiny ledge of a foothold may be the only sliver of silver lining in a dark, terrible storm cloud.

As spring arrived and sunlight lingered longer I had felt a subtle buoying of sorts, and the head dunking eased a little. It was the first time I had had perspective of any kind for eight months. The small change was magnified by the contrast of hopelessness. I had found a brief foothold in the pit.

I would love to say that this was the beginning of the climb out into the sunlight and I could look back at the hole and feel relieved that I had escaped and could move on with my life. Unfortunately, this story repeated itself for five years in a row. In the spring I would get a breath, and as soon as the nights began to cool down and autumn flavored the air with dying smells and red leaves I would slip back into the pit. The first tastes of the slipping were the hardest. The feeling and fear of the fall and the anticipation of the familiar horror at the bottom were almost too much to bear. After the pattern of rapid autumnal decline into the abyss my mind began to multiply the dread with the anxiety of its arrival. The season of fall began to mean the *verb* fall and I wasn't sure if I could endure another one.

I tried different medications. I tried different combinations of medications. I tried different therapists, doctors, scriptures, and websites. I tried ice water, UV lights, and hypnosis. I learned some tools to help deal with the darkness and the horror, but I wanted to find a way to stay out in the sunlight. There had to be a way, my spring mind would tell me. Then my depressed mind would fall back into the oblivion of hopelessness and sorrow—treading water and enduring the head dunking until the tiny foothold of spring emerged again. I knew deep down that this pattern could not be my life forever. If it became that way I eventually wouldn't survive it. My spring mind pleaded for me to hold on until help arrived, but my experiences and hopelessness in the pit were taking it's toll and each trip down was to a new bottom that seemed impossibly deeper. At some point there would be no foothold.

Back in the car, I decided to listen to some music, in celebration of the longer days and spring sunlight. The car cruised gently down the winding valley toward the small town in the distance. I turned the volume up loud to compete with the wind in my ears. It was a happy island rhythm with a catchy guitar riff--and what was that, maybe a flute? Very nice. As I listened to the singer the voice changed from the tropical ethnic accent to a twangy country-western voice. Strange, but nice, I thought. Then the lyrics materialized in my mind.

"There is nothing as sweet as your own homegrown. So green, so clean, you been there on the scene, ever since you were a little seed, yeah." It was Mishka and Willie Nelson singing about growing your own weed. I knew that song. Island rhythm and outlaw country combining to sing of the joys of home-grown cannabis.

"No way," I thought. "A ganja song—now? On the radio? What are the chances?" Normally the radio only picked up country or western, but this spot in the valley somehow magnified the signal of the community radio station in Salt Lake City, KRCL.

The Voice had been silent, perhaps letting the music do the talking. The junipers and sage blew gently in the breeze.

"I say, I say, there is nothing as sweet as your own homegrown. Free up the earth," played the music. I began tapping my thumbs to the rhythm. This was weird. I eased off of the gas. The speedometer was creeping up steadily with the downhill grade, and I had not noticed I was speeding. My left elbow was hanging out of the window and my arm hairs were vibrating in the wind, causing an itch. I rotated my arm enough to check the time. I scratched. The digits read 4:20. Four twenty.

"It is not a coincidence, dude," The Voice reemerged. "You can pretend it is, but this is inspiration. Can't you see it? Can't you feel it?" I wasn't quite sure what to think. "Do you know what day it is today?" the Voice asked.

"Thursday."

"No, Dude, the date."

"Look on you watch. It is April 20th—a fine spring day. If you write that out on paper it is 4/20. Coincidence? I think not, man."

Once again, my mind reeled. How could this be? Voices, feelings, times and dates? Who was this I was conversing with? This did not make any sense. Yet it made complete sense.

I slammed on the brakes and pulled off onto the muddy gravel shoulder of the road. I shook my head quickly, trying to get ahold of my thoughts.

"What is going on here? This is turning into a Twilight Zone episode."

"Don't you think Joseph Smith thought the same thing while he was kneeling in the woods in New York? Of course, the Twilight Zone, and TV for that matter, was still a hundred years away—but I bet he was freaked out too, man."

"I need to think this through," I said. "Give me some time, please."

"You have until this drive is over, and then I disappear and leave you alone in this cold and dreary world." I began driving again, pulling slowly onto the highway, no cars whatsoever in the rear-view mirror. The sound of mud and gravel flipping up from the wet shoulder of the road sounded like distant automatic gunfire as I regained speed and headed south.

Finally, I spoke up, "By the way, why is 4-20 a code word for weed, anyway?"

"I'm not sure. Google it, dude. I think it has something to do with some pot smoker kids lighting up at that time in the afternoon."

I thought about how to interpret the message and where these feelings and voice were coming from—on high, or from my worldly sub-consciousness, the natural man.

I was always a little skeptical of people who prayed and reported answers with a sign—maybe a rainbow or a voice like Morgan Freeman's coming out of the blue. It seemed like the scriptures were full of stories of prayers being answered by being knocked out or visited by heavenly messengers, but that never seemed to happen to me. Until now.

I had a friend who would pray for answers in life and then blindly stick her finger into the scriptures and get the solutions from the exact word or verse she was "led" to. Another more modern friend hit shuffle on his IPod and let the song lyrics answer his prayer. Obviously, your taste in music would affect your answers I told him. If you only have the Mormon Tabernacle Choir on your playlist your answers are going to be different than Snoop Dog and Jay Z.

The muddy gravel had spun off and the road was gently winding through the valley. The radio had turned to static and I turned it off to concentrate.

I turned the final curve and began the straightaway toward town, distant on the horizon. I focused on pushing the thought of autumn away and concentrated on the warm, spring light on my face and wind in my ears. I was almost back home. The sun was nearly down, but was still bright, daylight savings having sprung forward and the days getting longer.

I decided I would take a slight detour once I got to town and head to the church. I could park in front, turn off the engine, and pray for guidance once more. A messenger of evil may seem convincing in a worldly context, or listening to the radio, but I guessed near a church I could be more in tune with the spirit of light and goodness.

"I hear there is a great burger joint in your town. Is that true? Bacon cheese burgers? Kent's Kountry Kitchen? You should tell him the cute country spelling is unfortunate and actually not *that* cute." The Voice was back.

I replied, "Yep. How did you know about the burgers?"

"I know your thoughts, Bro," it continued. "I'm you. In you. You can't escape. Going to a church won't fix it."

"You are confusing me. I need clarity—guidance."

"OK. OK. I get it. But think about it. Maybe I am the clarity and the confusion is coming from your authorities being wrong."

"Or maybe not."

"Right on, bro. Touché. But maybe the purpose of life is you trying to figure this out and not just get the answers easily. Maybe if you look at the people who say the answers are easy you will find that they are easy for that person, but not for you. Or maybe they are lying."

"Honestly, I'd really just like someone to tell me what to do, make it easier—simplify it."

"Yeah, Dude. That sounds pretty good. But it also doesn't really make this trip you're on such a tough test, does it? Maybe the point is the struggle and what you can learn from it. Maybe the point is learning to think about others and not just your own darkness."

"You don't know how hard it is to think of anything or anyone when you are struggling to get your head above water," I complained.

"Maybe I do know how hard it is."

"Maybe you don't."

"Maybe I do. Remember—I am you, dude."

The car was entering the city limits and I began to take the detour west to the chapel.

"See you later, I guess?" I asked. There was no reply. "Dude? You there? You said I had until town to talk, right?" Nothing.

I turned left near the trailer park, an old black and white Aussie shepherd chasing my car as I slowed down to make the turn. The fruit trees were glowing white with small flowers and I breathed deeply through my nose with the first smells of life and spring.

The church building was catching the orange rays of sunset, the parking lot empty. I pulled in and turn the engine off, exhaling and trying to gain my bearings. I prayed silently. I reclined the seat and twisted my lumbar joints right and then left. Gazing out of the driver's side window I watched a fat robin hopping on the grass near the front door. It paused and looked at me for a moment, then hopped again and took to the air. Behind the bird the glass door reflected the burning sky and the mountains on the horizon. As the sun's last light disappeared under the purple and white peaks and my eyes rested on the bold address numbers posted on the brick next to the front door. A clear 4 and 2 and 0 marked the four hundred twenty north location of the chapel I had never noticed it before.

"Is that from you?" I asked. I took a deep breath and exhaled slowly. I closed my eyes. A bee buzzed near the car window. I sniffed, the hay fever setting in. Children laughed and played in the distance. A mom yelled for them to come in to eat dinner.

There was no answer.

THE PRICE I WOULD PAY

"What is our price limit to put him back together—you know, surgery or whatever?" Monica asked from the passenger seat, her eyes straight ahead on the road.

I hadn't thought about the money at all. I paused a few moments and realized I didn't have to debate anything in my mind. "There is no limit. I'll do what it takes."

"I should have closed the gate," she mumbled. "I looked out the window a minute before it happened and saw the gate open, but I didn't close it."

"It's not your fault. I've worried about that busy road since we first moved in. I always worried it would lead to Hayduke's demise."

"Pass this farmer truck already. He's going like 50 miles an hour."

I sped up with a clear view of the highway in front of us and passed the old pickup.

Only ten minutes earlier my heart dropped as I opened my cell phone and deciphered the text "haydukg0thit." I was in the middle a PowerPoint for new international student orientation, the first day of class, and my phone would not stop vibrating in my pocket. It buzzed and buzzed, until I finally figured it was something more important than discussing culture shock and reminding students that the legal drinking age in the US was 21. I left the class in a blur, and sweatily called Monica from my bike on the way home.

"Hayduke was chasing a pickup with some barking dogs in the back and he got hit by the truck," she moaned. "Come home fast."

I pedaled until my lungs and legs burned, riding through the intersection with the stop sign. My heart was pumping doubly from pedaling and adrenaline as I ditched the bike in the front yard and ran over to the dog. Mateo, my almost three year old, was yelling "Hayduke got hit by a caw and bwoke his weg. He's bweeding aw ovow."

I was intensely relieved to see Mateo healthy and Hayduke merely limping, and not a heap of fur and meat like the deer carcasses next to the frozen winter highways. The dog was whimpering and had a crushed foot, with some exposed bones and a slow oozing of blood, but he was alive. Fragile bodies versus tons of fast moving metal rarely have such fortunate outcomes. My nerves loosened a notch as the panic eased. I strained to pick up his spotted, 100 pound, half-Saint Bernard frame. I heaved, careful not to bump his flayed rear leg, and put him in the back of the car. "Let's go to the vet hospital," I said, lifting Mateo into his car seat, holding him for an extra second or two, and kissing him a gently on the top of his head.

MUD AND A HUNDRED DOLLARS

Rex Robideaux Lee had never seen so much mud in all of his life. Red mud. Mud that covered people's feet and sprayed the faces of the motorcycle drivers as they dodged potholes the size of Hondas. Mud just didn't exist in a nice curb and gutter city like Orinda, California where he grew up. It rained a bit, but there just wasn't time or room for mud.

Cambodia was different—about as different as Rex could get, which was why he was traveling there by bus from Bangkok for a week or so before heading to the islands, the girls, and the full moon parties. He wanted to go to a place his parents would freak out about. A place where there was still a bit of danger and mystery. A place with malaria and land mines and mud. To Rex, Cambodia was the right place.

He stepped up into an old Soviet truck with a wooden passenger compartment bolted to the back. There were already people sitting on every available inch of bench, so Rex stooped low and worked his way up to the front and made a seat out of his backpack. He was quite happy with the results. The wooden benches looked hard and oily anyway. The diesel engine turned over, firing up a green cloud of exhaust that immediately seeped into the open aired bus. Rex had the feeling it was going to be a long nine-hour ride to Phnom Penh.

Just as the vehicle was rolling out onto the soggy road another foreigner jumped on the back and worked his way up to where Rex sat. He had the look of a rugged traveler: worn bohemian clothing, a small daypack, short hair, and a weathered face. He was quite wet from walking through the monsoon rain, and his feet were red past his ankles.

"Ca va?" The traveler said as he set his pack down next to Rex. "English?"

"Yeah. How's it going? You just made the bus."

"I was running the last hundred meters." His French accent was quite strong, and it sounded, to Rex, like he swallowed the ends of his words. "I am very wet now."

"Yeah, I have a feeling this is going to be a long bus ride." The French guy began pulling a dry shirt from his pack and put it on.

"I agree. We will be lucky to make it in eight hours. Do you mind if I sit here next to you. There is no seat."

"No problem." Rex extended his hand. "My name is Rex. I'm from California."

"I am Jean Luc, like the captain in Star Trek. Is this your first time in Camboge?" He leaned back on the truck bed and sat cross-legged.

"Yeah."

"Your country dropped many bombs here. In secret."

"Yeah. We bombed the hell out of Cambodia and Laos I heard. And supposedly the war was just in Viet Nam. Look at it now out there— it really is almost like the Stone Age. Just like Johnson said, we bombed 'em back into it." Rex always felt strange talking about the US bombing nearly every country in South East Asia. "I also heard the French weren't much kinder than the Americans, though."

"There were many problems with the French here, too. It depends who tells you the story," Jean Luc replied.

"It usually does, doesn't it?" Rex and Jean Luc stared out of the window for a short time.

Finally, Jean Luc spoke up. "It is a sad, sad country with a horrible history, a lot of suffering. They say one person in 250 lost a limb and one in eight lost a family member. But still a very beautiful place if you can see through it."

"Yeah, I'm sure. If you can manage to stay away from the mines." Rex coughed the last of the diesel from his lungs.

"You want a smoke?" Rex pulled a pack of cigarettes out of his shirt pocket.

"Oui. Thank you." Jean Luc leaned back and watched the shanties and rice paddies slowly roll by, through the plastic wrapped sides of the vehicle.

"I haven't seen many Americans around here. A few Europeans, Japanese and Australians," he said.

"Yeah, the Americans are eating 'all you can eat' in a restaurant in Hawaii or Cancun for their vacation. Cambodia isn't exactly a top U.S. tourist destination."

"True. Many French people do the same. Tahiti, Nice. For me they are a bit boring. I like more adventure."

"Yeah." Rex exhaled slowly, blowing his smoke out into the muggy air. The road was completely dark minus the headlights of the truck, but occasionally they would pass a pair of blue-black florescent lights a top a plastic sheet. These strange outcroppings looked like glowing, alien sailboats floating on the rice paddies, each one guarded by a few villagers.

"What are those disco lights for?" Rex asked.

"The blue lights attract the crickets. They hit the plastic and fall down into buckets on the ground and the people collect them. They catch maybe 100 big crickets in a night."

"Should I ask why?"

"They are a delicacy. Roasted and salted. They taste like burned peanuts with legs." Jean Luc raised his eyebrows and made crunching sounds with his mouth, laughing.

"Sick." Rex leaned his head back against the cab until the bumps and potholes in the dirt road slammed the truck against it. "I have never been on a bus trip where my kidneys hurt from the bumps jarring me."

"Yeah, roads don't get much worse. And these are the best roads in the country. They used to be excellent when France controlled Indochina. Three or four wars later the roads are horrible." He pronounced it "orrible."

"I've been in a bus for almost two days now. I'm so tired I think I could actually sleep." Rex mumbled as he curled up around his backpack.

"Wake me up if we hit a land mine."

They stopped only once in the night, for the bus to fill up the fuel tank. The gas station was nothing more than a wooden shack next to the road with stacks of two liter Coke bottles filled with fuel. The bus drained a pile of bottles and continued its rattling down the road.

At daybreak the bus finally struck some pavement, which felt as smooth as butter to Rex after a night of bouncing and bruising in the truck bed. The transition woke him up and within half an hour the bus was in the station and the two travelers were hustled away to a run down guesthouse by a mad man of a cyclo driver. The cyclo was no more than a rusty two-wheeled cart bolted to the back of a Japanese motorbike. The man rushed Rex and Jean Luc off of the bus speaking in a mix of French and English about the "best hotel, best price, my friend, my friend." They were both ready for a plate of fried rice and a nap.

Upon arrival at the Akun guesthouse, the sweating travelers peeled themselves off of the vinyl seats of the cyclo and walked into the most beautiful thing they had seen in the country. She was sitting in the front office arranging the books. Her hair was still wet and hanging over her face, and when she looked up, it was as if the sun had risen for the second time that morning. Both Jean Luc and Rex stopped walking and stared. The girl looked up and smiled, a slow succulent smile, Buddha like, as she placed her hands together in front of her chin and bowed gracefully. Her almond shaped eyes were dark and her honey-brown skin was smooth and radiant. Neither Rex nor Jean Luc knew what to say. They were in the presence of a goddess. They stumbled, removing their shoes from the door.

"Do you have any rooms?" Jean Luc stammered.

The girl looked at a logbook on the desk. "Only one room left right now. But it has two beds. Or do you want one bed? We can move the beds together."

"Oh no. We are not together," Rex scoffed.

"We will have more rooms opening tomorrow. Would you like to share the room tonight?"

The guys talked it over and decided it would save money—on the other hand, there were ten other hotels around the block, desperate for business.

"OK, then." Jean Luc said as he walked out of the lobby. "It was nice to meet you. Good luck with your travels."

Rex put his backpack on and began walking the other way down the street. "Yeah, maybe we'll see each other around town. He waved good-bye, walked a block, and turned the corner only to run directly into the sun, humidity, and ripe stench of Phnom Penh. Even before that moment Rex realized he didn't want another hotel. He didn't want a better room. He wanted to see that girl again.

Rex wiped the sweat off of his forehead with his shirtsleeve and made a 180-degree turn. He marched back to the guesthouse lobby reciting "hello" in Khmer from his pocket phrase book.

When he reentered the lobby his mouth fumbled the words, not only because the syllables were so awkward, but because Jean Luc was already sitting next to the front desk and the Cambodian princess was smiling her beautiful smile as he rambled on in French.

"Well it didn't take you long to come back," Rex commented quickly.

"I looked around the block, but this place is much better. It didn't take you long to look either, no?" He was grinning at Rex.

"No. It's too damn hot to walk around."

"I feel the same. Let's share the room. OK?"

"Fine. At this point I don't care." Rex fanned himself with his phrase book. But, Rex did care. He cared for the most beautiful thing in Cambodia no matter how hot and smelly the country was.

"OK. It's a deal."

The travelers lounged a bit in the lobby area, looking at paintings, buying a few crispy snack crackers, and talking to the girl. Soon they walked up the stairs, set their packs down, and sat down with the fan on high circling above. Rex laughed out loud and took a swallow of a sweaty Anchor beer he bought in the lobby. He sat on the edge of the bed tapping his feet like a drummer.

"What is so funny?" Jean Luc was chuckling too, now.

"You know what is so funny, you suave Frenchman."

"You also came back for the little beauty, no?"

"Of course I did. So did you." Rex took another swallow from the bottle and handed it over to Jean Luc.

"It's a little bit early for beer, but I could use some, yes." Jean Luc poured a bit into a glass from the table and passed the bottle back. Rex was still laughing out loud, tapping his feet, and making little musical sounds with his lips. "Why are you so happy? The girl likes me."

"You pompous Frenchman. She hasn't even met me. You don't stand a chance." Rex was speeding up his rhythm.

"Stupid American. You think the world is yours to plunder. You have no idea." Jean Luc kidded.

"You ave no idea." Rex mocked back, laughing. "But, I do have an idea. Are you a wagering man? How about a bet? Me and you. Mano a mano, or whatever." He looked at Jean Luc. "Whoever scores with the chic first, wins."

"You are disgusting. I cannot believe you would say such a thing."

"Why? It's in good fun. Just a bet."

"It is immoral," Jean Luc paused. "And you will lose."

"One hundred dollars says I won't," Rex whispered, and ceased his rhythmic motions. He took another swallow of his breakfast beer and looked over at the Frenchman. "One hundred dollars. America versus France. May the best man win."

Jean Luc took a slow sip and shook his head again. "You make me sick, but I must prove you wrong. Stupid American. We have a deal."

Rex Robideaux Lee showered in a freezing blast of water that was more of a metal hose coming out of the bathroom wall than a shower. He struggled to get his hair wet because the water hit him in the middle of the chest. The toilet hole, sink, and shower were all cramped in a small cinderblock and plaster room at the end of the hall.

He changed clothes into an aloha shirt, camouflage cotton shorts, and flip flops, slicked back his blond hair, and splashed on a bit of travel sized Polo aftershave to cut through the traveler mildew stink on everything he owned. It was well into the afternoon now, and after a nap Rex felt refreshed. He was ready to begin seeing the town and make his moves on the girl.

Gaek, which meant "jade" in Khmer, Rex later found out, was still at the front desk, studying a book on English vocabulary. She looked up when he walked down the stairs.

"Hello," Rex said, glancing at the book. "It looks like you're practicing your English."

"Yes. I have a class every Saturday to learn." She was shy, but still always smiling underneath her timid eyes.

"I can teach you a few things, if you want," Rex replied, pushing his hair behind his ear. "I'm a bit of an expert in English."

She smiled again. I have one question. Does the subject always come before the verb and object in a sentence?"

Rex was dumbfounded. He never had to learn grammar after the fourth grade. "Hmm." He tried to look confident. "Yes. I would say, yes." He paused. "English is crazy, you see. Do you know what we call a group of fish?"

"Fish?"

"Yeah, fish. A group of fish is called a school. Like where you go to study. And a group of wolves is a pack. Weird, huh?" Rex was on a roll. Gaek look absolutely amazed. "Can I take you to dinner tonight, and we can talk about more English?" Rex risked being blunt. Gaek looked down at the floor. "We can even eat here at the hotel if you're nervous. I mean, with your family and friends around," Rex continued.

She twirled a pencil on the desk. "I would like to go, but I am already going to eat dinner with your friend. He asked me a little while ago."

"Oh, OK," Rex tried to look fine with the fact that Jean Luc was stealing his girl already. "No worries. Let's try for tomorrow?"

"Yes. I would love to practice English tomorrow," she beamed. "I will be here."

Rex nodded. "Great. Tomorrow." He walked out into the warm afternoon rain without any umbrella or rain jacket. He just wanted to walk around in the mud for a while.

The moment Rex stepped out into the street he was surrounded by men on motorbikes asking him if he wanted a ride.

"Where you go? I take you. Best price. Best price, my friend," shouted the first guy to get to him. He was a thin man with several long strands of chin hair and a worn out t-shirt.

"No, thanks. I'm just going to walk," replied Rex loudly. "I'm walking around. That is all." He continued through the crown of men and strolled briskly down the garbage-strewn road.

"I take to the killing fields. Pol Pot's house. Airport." The man was still following him down the street on his motorbike.

"No." Rex continued to walk. He stumbled then, almost falling in the gurgling open grey water of the sewer next to him. He recovered and shook his head. "Screw it," he mumbled out loud. "OK. Give me a ride downtown. Take me to a good restaurant or something."

"OK, friend." The driver pulled over and Rex jumped on the back. "Where you from? I will show you the town. Good tour, and then we go to the Dragon Restaurant."

"Great. Let's go." Rex held on to the back of the bike for his life as the driver swerved through motos, tuk-tuks, bikes, chickens, and dogs all merging at intersections with no traffic signs. "It's like playing Frogger with your life around here," Rex said.

"What?"

"Nothing."

The motorbike driver drove out of town for ten minutes and pulled into an alley that opened up at the back into a large field. Two men on either side of the road signaled the driver in. At first, to Rex, it looked like a driving range without any golfers. There was rough grass, a couple of targets to aim at, and a protected area where a few men sat around on folding metal chairs and drooping hammocks.

"This doesn't look like a restaurant," Rex spoke up.

"Oh, this is much better. We'll go to the restaurant next." The driver parked his bike under a rusting tin roof. "Let's choose a weapon."

"What?" Rex moved nervously behind the driver as the men stood up and walked to a large wooden box and opened the lid.

Inside the box were more guns than Rex had ever seen. He had shot at clay pigeons once with his uncle Larry in Reno with a 12 gauge shotgun, but these guns looked much more steely and ominous.

"AK-47's price is $20 for 50 bullets. Pistols are $10 to shoot." The driver seemed to be in on the business and Rex wondered how many other travelers he had brought there. "The best, of course, is the rocket launcher here. It is $40 to shoot one rocket." As he said this, another man opened a wooden box full of conical shapes, displaying the rusty arsenal of RPGs.

Rex was uneasy, to say the least, but he also felt the rush of excitement. He had never seen such power so close to his fingertips. If he shot off a few rounds he would have a very cool story to tell to his friends back home. The men all turned to look at the foreigner.

"Let's try the AK-47," Rex spoke loudly.

"Good idea."

One man got out of the hammock and walked out in the field as another prepared the gun for firing. Rex watched as the man in the field unveiled two human looking dummies, stuffed with straw. One was dressed in the black ninja clothing, with a red and white scarf of the Khmer Rouge, the other was dressed in military fatigues, the face a photocopy of Arnold Schwarzenegger. The Cambodian holding the stock of the Russian AK-47 began laughing and pointing at the targets.

"You can choose one to shoot," He chuckled.

Rex thought it was a bit strange to be shooting a real gun at a mannequin. Clay pigeons were one thing, but a dressed up doll with the face of a movie star? Rex figured it must be revenge for many South East Asians who undoubtedly watched movies with muscled Americans shooting their way through hundreds of look-alike men in black pajamas. He decided he would shoot at the governor of California and play it safe. Who knew how many of the men lounging around were part of the real death squads of Pol Pot anyway, Rex thought. He lifted the barrel skyward, aimed, and fired half of the clip, the weapon quickly recoiling upward.

"Wow," Rex said, completely in shock from the power of a fully automatic assault weapon. "I didn't hit a thing." He realized he had been closing his eyes the entire time. He opened them now and fired off a few more rounds without flinching so much. By the time he finished the bullets, Rex had torn apart the mid-section of the dummy completely. His body was vibrating with the buzz of violence, and Rex considered a shot at the rocket launcher.

"You want to try the *big daddy*?" The driver had seen Rex eyeing the weaponry.

"I'd like to," He paused. "But one shot is the same price at seven nights in the guest house." Rex knew he should get back to town, and he now had a good story to tell his friends. He motioned to the driver and paid him a twenty-dollar bill. The men all resumed their positions on their chairs and hammocks.

"What a country," Rex said from the back of the motorbike as they drove back toward town. He couldn't believe his luck, finding a driver that would take him all around the city for just a few dollars.

Rex ate a bowl of thick noodles with pieces of chopped, bony chicken at the Dragon Restaurant, chatting with his new friend about the New York Yankees. He didn't even know they cared about baseball in Cambodia, but the motorcycle driver knew every player on the team.

That night Rex returned to the hotel room to find Jean Luc's stuff gone and a note on the cracked bamboo table that said: *I'm in room four. Meet me at the Sunset Bar at 11:00 tonight to discuss bet.*

It was only 9:30, so Rex took another cold shower to break out of the spell cast by the constant heat. He had no idea where the Sunset Bar was, but he knew that the Frenchman had the advantage of the first date. This worried him a little, but Rex consoled himself with the fact that he was an American and had Hollywood and rock-and-roll on his side.

He looked for his moto-taxi friend outside the guest house, but couldn't find the man. Another driver said he knew the Sunset Bar so Rex jumped on back of the bike and they sped away into the heavy, wet air, hitting pockets of strong smells all the way into the town. The first odor was old moss, then roasted garlic, followed by rotting fish, and finally wood smoke with a hint of wet dog.

"I'll wait for you here," said the second driver. It's not safe to take taxis late at night here. Don't walk anywhere. There are men with guns."

Rex thought it was a bit ironic to hear these words from a taxi driver.

The Sunset Bar seedy, run down, and lowly lit with red and blue neon lighting. A middle aged, balding Cambodian sat in the middle of the bar with a keyboard and a mike, singing a Lionel Ritchie song with a terrible accent. Rex was not impressed with the place. He spotted Jean Luc drinking a Carlsberg at the corner table and pulled up a chair.

"Nice place," Rex smirked.

"It was once the place to come—in the colonial days of Indochina," Jean Luc said, swirling his cigarette and making puffy shaped smoke clouds in the dingy air. "It is quite run down now—but you can get the sense that it was very nice once."

"Yeah. In 1952." Rex lit up a Marlboro and ordered a Coke. He had a bit of a stomachache and his theory about Coke was that it would fix almost any tropical disease. Rex heard that a Coke could be used to clean a toilet and could eat away a nail or a penny if you left it in a glass overnight. If this was true, he figured Coke would kill any microbes or bugs that might harm his digestive tract.

"So how was dinner? You beat me to the first date, you sly dog."

"What is it you say? 'You snooze, you are a loser?' You were sleeping. I had to seize the moment." Jean Luc smiled and leaned forward in his chair.

"She is a very nice girl. I cannot go on with this stupid contest. It is not right."

"What?" Rex leaned back and blew smoke up toward the slowly turning fan on the ceiling. "I haven't even had a chance to meet the girl. You can't quit already.

"I am not quitting. I'm just saying it is stupid."

"Oh, I see," Rex paused. "You are playing the saint here because you know after one date that you're going to lose."

"Impossible. You pompous American. I am from the city of love."

"Then pay me now or else stick with the bet. The original bet."

"This is stupid. You will lose," Jean Luc smiled and looked out at the bar sprinkled with slender prostitutes and sweating, overweight tourist men. "OK, take your chance."

"Take my chance?" Rex laughed. "You just lost your chance Frenchy. The girl is mine now." They finished their drinks and walked outside to find a moto-taxi to get back.

When Rex spotted the motorbike driver he could tell there was something wrong. The man had a strange look in his eyes and before Rex could walk over to him in the crowd the man was on his bike and gone, trailing a cloud of exhaust.

"There goes my ride," Rex shouted. Jean Luc pulled his arm to get Rex out of the street as a tuk-tuk sped by, nearly clipping Rex's shoulder.

"There are taxis everywhere," Jean Luc motioned. "Be careful on the street. You were almost run over."

"Eh, my friend," A voice squealed from behind them. Rex spun around and saw it was the man from earlier that day with the Fu Manchu chin hairs. He was smiling and cleaning the long fingernail on his smallest finger. "I will give you a ride back to the hotel," he said. "My friend here has a motorbike to give your friend a ride, too."

Rex nodded in agreement, happy to get out of the street and the crowd near the bar. As they sped back to the Akun Guest House the driver spoke up quite loudly. At first Rex thought he was just speaking over the sound of the traffic, but the tone had an edge to it.

"Why did you ride with someone else tonight? I said I would take you. I thought we were friends," the driver said. Rex was a bit confused. The man's face was now snarled and cold in the rear view mirror.

"I looked for you," Rex apologized.

"I was only one minute late," His face was harsh still, and Rex began to feel agitated.

"Look, I'm sorry. I just didn't see you. Forget about it."

"I will not forget it. I said I would give you a ride. I'm a good driver. I'm your friend."

At this point the man turned around and produced a smile. The Rex it looked more like a stray dog showing its teeth as a warning, but he forced a laugh.

"It's OK. Next time I'll give you a ride. It's dangerous with other drivers. No worries with me." He turned his head back to face the oncoming traffic that at midnight seemed nearly as busy as midday. Rex's mind was swimming at how fast a place or a person could go from being so helpful to threatening so quickly. He recalled the scared look on the other driver's face at the bar and realized he must have been intimidated by Mr. Fu Manchu. Each was fighting for money to survive, Rex thought. The thin veneer of hospitality was momentarily broken, revealing the war torn, brutal center underneath. That raw and rugged inside was what it took for survivors of genocide to compete with their peers in the twenty first century in the stifling heat of South East Asia, Rex thought. It was simply survival of the fittest.

The next evening when Gaek got off work she met Rex in the restaurant outside of the guesthouse. It was an open-air place with a high thatched roof of finely woven palm fronds. The stereo played a mix of heavy metal ballads from the nineties and only one of the five tables had any customers. *Sweet Child of Mine* was playing softly as Rex serpentined his was to the small table and pulled the chair out for his gorgeous companion. Gaek was dressed in her usual cotton shirt and jeans, only with high platform flip-flops, looking quite modern. Her soft hair was pulled back, and she needed no make up or beautifying to look stunning.

Rex, in his only outfit other than a t-shirt, couldn't keep his eyes off of her.

"What is it like in America?" Gaek asked as Rex opened the menu. "Like the movies?"

"Well, kind of." Rex looked down at the menu, consciously trying not to stare any more than humanly possible. "It depends what movies. I suppose it is somewhere between Forrest Gump and Spider Man. But that is Hollywood. America is a big place. It's hard to say." Rex knew he wasn't making any sense, but his heart was coming out of his mouth and his brain was spinning in the presence of such exquisite perfection. "What is good to eat here?" Rex finally thought to ask.

"Do you like Cambodian food?"

"I don't know. I like noodles and rice."

"Why don't you try chicken curry with vegetables? It is quite flavorful. The cook can make it not-so-spicy for you."

"Oh no. I can eat spicy food." Rex snapped at the waiter. "I'll take the chicken curry. Regular spicy." The waiter nodded.

Gaek spoke to the waiter in Khmer--ordering something, Rex guessed.

"My uncle lives in the United States now," Gaek continued. "He escaped from the Khmer Rouge and lived in Thailand in a refugee camp. Now he works in a restaurant in Vermont."

"Really? You should go and visit," Rex said.

"I'd really love to go, but it is not easy. It is difficult to get a visa and very expensive."

"Yeah, I bet. But you can save money and maybe your uncle can help you."

"Yes. I'm saving money now. One dollar at a time. Is that how you say it?" Gaek asked.

"Your English is really good Gaek, I don't know why you think you need lessons in school."

"It needs to be better," she said as the waiter placed two steaming plates of rice and two colorful bowls of fragrant red curry on the table.

"This smells really good," Rex said, driving a spoon into the bowl and scooping up a healthy bite of fresh vegetables. It took six seconds for the heat of the curry to hit Rex full force, and by that time he had spooned another mouthful down and swallowed the whole thing. The burn hit him in the stomach first and radiated up through his throat to his mouth. He reached for the bottle of water on the table, but there was no relief.

"Are you OK?" Gaek asked as Rex began to cry and hiccup uncontrollably.

"Fine. Fine," he squeaked miserably.

"Eat some rice if the curry is too spicy," she whispered.

"I'm OK," Rex lied and ate huge spoonfuls of rice as inconspicuously as possible. He couldn't really talk. He had eaten hot things before, but never something that kept burning for so long.

After about five minutes Rex could speak again and the rest of the evening went splendidly well, in his opinion. He got to know about Gaek by asking about her family—he knew girls loved that. She continued to ask question after question about America, which in Rex's mind meant he was scoring some major points.

As they sat there a small group of amputees and beggars gathered on the corner, across the street. For several minutes Rex watched the crowd as they huddled together outside. Suddenly, another group of several uniformed police or security men pushed through the handicapped men, hitting them with long sticks and shouting at them like stray dogs. The crowd dispersed, hobbling away from the street in all directions.

"What was that?" Rex asked. "Did you see that?"

"Those people were waiting for the tourist bus to come into town. When the tourists get off it is the beggars' best chance to get money for food. The tourists have so much more money than anyone here." Gaek continued, "The store owners don't want the tourists to get upset and stay inside their hotels. They want people to spend money and walk in the safe streets, so they pay men to keep the street clean."

"That doesn't seem right to me, hitting those men."

"It isn't right, but it is what needs to happen right now. There is no money here and we need tourist business." Gaek responded.

Shortly after, the tourist bus pulled up to the corner, unloading a handful of travelers several minutes later. Rex looked casually through the window as they were whisked away on different motorcycle taxis or searched for hotels, their Lonely Planet guidebooks in hand.

The date ended with Gaek telling Rex that she needed to get to her nighttime English course. Rex tried to make the excuse that she was getting a more effective one on one lesson with him, be she wouldn't listen to him.

"Maybe tomorrow night for dinner? We could go out and eat at another restaurant—wherever you want to go." Rex pleaded. "I won't take no for an answer. You need the English practice." He smiled.

Gaek finally told him that she actually had plans to meet with Jean Luc for dinner, but she paused and said maybe she could see him another time. She looked awkwardly at the floor.

"Just tell him you are busy with another appointment. He'll understand." Rex sniffed, feeling the dull ache in his stomach that was far from finished.

"But I already told him it was OK." She began to waver. Rex could feel her being polite and helped her reconsider.

"Just tell him you'll meet for tea or lunch and then come and meet me."

"Maybe." She was swaying and beginning to smile a little again.

"Come on," Rex touched her hand gently under the table. She blinked slowly and adjusted her necklace.

"OK. Tomorrow night. Can we talk about America some more?"

"Excellent. I'll see you tomorrow." Rex left confidently, feeling his charming skills were at their zenith.

When he got to his room there was another note on the door to meet Jean Luc at the Sunset Bar. Rex was out of the guesthouse and on the moto-taxi with the Fu Manchu driver in less than ten minutes. He had news to discuss.

Two men were loudly arguing at the bar when Rex walked in. He saw Jean Luc sitting at a table in the corner of the room, but the only way to get to the table was to walk right next to the two angry men. They looked somehow official—they weren't in uniform, but they carried themselves with authority. Rex didn't want to make trouble, so he half-bowed and slid by the men to reach the table and Jean Luc

Both men stopped their grunting and gazed at the foreigner from head to toe, staring jadedly, as he walked by. Rex sat down quickly as Jean Luc peeling the wet label off of the bottle in front of him.

"You need to be careful of men like that," Jean Luc commented. "They look like trouble. See the bulge near the back pocket of the larger man?"

Rex turned around slowly and nodded.

"He is carrying a pistol. The other guy has one too, I bet."

"What was I supposed to do? I had to get by."

"I'm only saying to be careful of men like that," Jean Luc commenced his ripping of the label and placed it on the table.

"Why don't you be careful yourself? Everyone is always telling me to be careful. I'm sick of it. The only way to be careful is to go home." Rex breathed in the stale air and turned back toward Jean Luc. "By the way. Gaek? She wants me." He was smiling now. "She is completely infatuated with me."

"You sound so sure."

"I am. It's only a matter of days." Rex looked up as a shadow was cast over the table from the direction of the bar. The large Cambodian man was towering over the table, his leathery hands on his hips. He began speaking loudly and motioning violently with his hands extended toward Rex. He was stocky for a Cambodian, though not as tall as Rex, and his eyes held a glaze that was more than simply anger or alcohol. Rex couldn't understand a word of what he was saying, but it was obviously not friendly.

Once again, to Rex, the veil between a needy tourist country and the terror of intimidation had become a little bit too transparent.

"Get up," the shorter man, with the pistol in his belt, yelled.

"Why do you wear those pants?" He pointed at Rex's camouflaged shorts. "Do you mock us? Our army?" Both men had transfixed their anger toward the American.

"I mean no disrespect. No problems." Rex was standing now, in shock, and he held his hands up high. "They are just my shorts. Lots of people wear camo."

"Come outside now!" The short man pulled a pistol from behind his back and waved it at Rex and Jean Luc. "Both of you, outside!"

Rex and Jean Luc hunched over and slowly walked toward the door, their hands up and their eyes nervously scanning their situation. Everyone else in the bar watched the event in silence, stepping back out of the way and pretending not to be alarmed.

"We want no problems," Jean Luc began to explain, but he was cut off immediately by both men behind him.

"Shut up." The large man kicked him in the back.

"Walk."

Outside the bar the men motioned for the foreigners to stand in the middle of the street.

"Take off your clothes!" Both men now pointed pistols at Rex.

"You." They pointed at Jean Luc. "You give us your money and you can go."

Terrified with visions of brutal executions, Rex began shaking uncontrollably. He pleaded to be released.

"I am sorry about the shorts. I don't mean any harm. Take my money," he sobbed. Rex's mind was spinning. "How could this be happening? He thought to himself. It was all a mistake. He meant these people no harm. A stabbing pain of nausea hit him and Rex questioned what in the hell he was even doing in that country, let alone that situation. He should have been on the beach somewhere getting sunburned.

Jean Luc passed the dollar bills in his pocket to the smaller man and slowly backed into the crowd while the attention was on Rex.

"Take off your pants. Now!" The thick guy cocked the hammer of his small, black pistol.

"No." Rex screamed. "Don't shoot!" He dropped his shorts and boxers and kicked them off as he pulled his shirt over his head and tossed it into the street.

This motion caused a chuckle from the armed men. Rex stood naked in his flip-flops.

"You won't mock us now," The man said, tossing his gun back and forth between his hands. Rex tried in vain to cover himself. He whimpered in a mix of humiliation and fear, trying not to soil himself.

The men spoke loudly to each other in Khmer and Jean Luc watched quietly from the shadows near the moto-taxis. The men turned back to Rex and the small man leveled his gun. The crowd was silent in an instant. Rex breathed in and raised his hands again.

"Bang! Bang! Go home," said the small man, who found the situation hilarious and began to laugh uncontrollably. Rex picked up his shorts and sprinted down the street toward the hotel. The small crowd dispersed as the two armed men tucked the pistols in their pants and returned to the bar.

Jean Luc, hiding in the periphery, spied the moto-taxi driver with the Fu Manchu beard and pulled him into the shadows. "Where can we find the police?" He asked, still trembling and looking around nervously.

"You just saw the police," the taxi driver replied. "They were the men with the guns. You should stay away from them. Wait until they leave the area and I'll give you a ride." His head dropped, his eyes scanning the ground around the motorbikes. "It is dangerous for me if they see us together now."

Jean Luc sat in the alley for half an hour in silence until the taxi driver returned and said it was safe. They rode back to the guesthouse, and Jean Luc quickly ran upstairs. He knocked on Rex's door hard, and the door opened when he touched it. He entered carefully, calling out Rex's name.

The room was empty, except for a pair of camouflaged shorts lying in the corner. Jean Luc ran back downstairs and found Gaek hiding in a small room behind the front desk. She was sobbing wildly, her eyes red and puffy.

"He's gone." She mumbled. "He wouldn't even speak to me. He just ran out and I know he isn't coming back."

"Is there a bus leaving tonight?" Jean Luc asked sternly.

The girl's natural beauty still radiated through the tear streaked face, and for the first time since they met he noticed that she wasn't smiling.

"There is a bus to Poi Pet at midnight. And Rex told me to tell you you won. I don't even know what he was talking about. He will never take me to Vermont now."

Jean Luc paused, wiping a tear from the Gaek's cheek. It's not your fault. We had a bad experience with the police tonight. Rex was scared. They almost shot him and they took my money." He paused, looking down at the floor. "I'm leaving too, Gaek. I'm sorry. But, I just might make the bus if I leave right now." Jean Luc rushed upstairs to pack his things.

WHERE YOU ARE

"Where am I?" Lenny asked the gas station attendant with an upward jerk of his shoulders. The man looked up, socket wrench in his greased and oily hand, and pushed the brim of his baseball hat back on his forehead.

"*Where* you are is a simple answer, friend, but *why* you are here seems a bit more perplexing to me." He held the socket end of the wrench and swirled the handle leisurely in circles like he was winding an enormous clock. "Of course I'm speaking of the metaphysical 'why', not a simple geographical locale."

There was a slight pause, and he continued. "You are in Brinkersville, Wyoming, home of the Willard County Fair, which just so happens to start this weekend. Welcome. But again I ask you—why are you here?"

Lenny had no idea why he was Brinkersville, or how he ended up in a place where everyone had a bucking bronco on their license plate. It had been eleven whole months since he'd had any sort of episode like this. He thought something miraculous had happened and he was cured. Obviously, that wasn't the case at all.

"I'll tell you why you are here," the mechanic rambled on. "You are a child of your father in heaven and he has something in store for you. It wasn't simply happenstance that placed you on this planet at this time in history."

"Hold on a second," Lenny said.

"You are here for a reason. Do you want to know why?" The man wiped his nose with the back of his sleeve and left a greasy smear across his cheek.

Lenny blinked slowly, trying to get his bearings on the situation. "Did you say Brinkersville?"

"Man, are you listening to me? I'm telling you the secret to life and we aren't even on the same page."

"I'm sorry. It's just that I'm a bit lost."

"I'll say you are lost. But what shepherd wouldn't leave ninety nine sheep to find the lost one?" The man said, digging some dirt out from under his fingernail.

"I'm telling you where you are—in the plan, man. You're in the *plan*." The gas station man was beginning to bounce around on the gravel a bit now, and Lenny turned the key of his Ford Taurus.

"You owe me twenty-two dollars for the gas, friend." The man began twirling the socket wrench around again, his other hand planted firmly on the driver's side windowsill.

"Sorry," Lenny mumbled, sitting up and stretching out to reach in his pocket. He paid the man. "I've got this little problem where I—I lose track of time and forget where I am sometimes. I haven't had any issues for some time now, but I guess it has happened again." Lenny had no idea why he was telling a complete stranger about his issues.

"Well, we all get a little lost at times. That's why we need to follow the path." The mechanic leaned down to Lenny's eye level. "You know what I mean? Wouldn't you like to know more?"

Lenny turned his eyes toward the windshield. "Thanks, but I'm not really interested in your plan right now."

"How can you not be interested? If Jesus came down in a blaze of glory and had the answers for you wouldn't you want to hear them?" He said.

"I don't believe it is quite that easy." Lenny replied. "I just want to know where I am."

"I'm telling you where you are." The gasman was squeezing the windowsill now and Lenny shifted into drive.

"I've got to get going. Thanks for your help, Mr."

As he sped out of the gas station and onto the dusty road Lenny heard the man yelling, "You are part of the plan, man!" The sagebrush passed by in a blur, and Lenny rolled up the window.

STOUFFER'S SPICY SALSA

When Julio and Mary Beth were engaged it was the first romance that the Stouffers Frozen Dinner factory could officially take credit for. There were dates and secret love affairs, of course, but never a full-fledged wedding of employees in 27 years. They met on the vegetable line. Julio was monitoring a huge vat of green beans. Mary Beth was measuring creamed corn. Mary Beth's facemask slipped down off of one ear, nearly falling into the corn, and Julio looked across the machinery just in time to catch a glimpse of a small star-shaped birthmark above her lip. It was that purplish star that drew him to her like a trout to a silvery, sparkling lure.

Julio finally summoned up the courage to ask Mary Beth out for Mexican food. He knew a nice little restaurant with excellent enchiladas and as much hot, homemade salsa as one could handle. Mary Beth was delighted to be asked out for dinner. She hadn't gone on a date since the second season of *Friends*, and that date was a less-than-impressive blind one with her cousin's friend and four other people.

Julio picked Mary Beth up at her house in his Toyota Corolla. It wasn't much of a car to look at, but it was nearly paid off and the gas mileage was good. He checked his hair in the rear view and brushed down his thin mustache with his thumbnail. He was feeling a touch over-the-hill that night—not old, but just that ache in the knees and shine on temples where the hair was edging back a bit. After a quick check for anything lodged in his teeth Julio gave himself a little wink and sprang out of the car with a little shuffle step in the gravel.

Mary Beth answered the door quickly, smelling fresh, and slammed the door behind her.

"Let's get outta here," she whispered, walking away, knowing that her mother would be at the front window watching her leave. Her mother didn't like Julio. She didn't know him, but she didn't like him. No one would be good enough for her Mary Beth.

The restaurant was lit up with bright colored lights and little paper flags that had skeletons cut out of them. It smelled spicy and alive inside. Julio and Mary Beth got a booth near the back and ordered combination meals that came on hot oval plates the waiter could barely lift. The music was ripe with a tenor's vibrato and a rhythmic tuba.

I'm sorry I said your name wrong when I first met you," Mary Beth said. "I'm not used to the Mexican pronunciation."

"Don't worry. It's no problem." He drank some of his piña colada from a glass the size of a birdbath, and took a deep breath. "What would you do if you weren't working at Stouffers?" He stirred his straw.

"Me? I'd be a movie director or something. Science fiction movies. You know, like Star Trek. But like the old Star Trek, not the new one. I'd create new space creatures that looked like humans, but they would have different parts like strange foreheads or weird colored eyes or pointy ears. That's what I'd do. Maybe not be a director, but a make-up artist."

"How about you?" she asked.

He looked up briefly at the paper flags.

"A pilot, I hope. I'm not going to be working at Stouffers for long. It's just temporary until I get my money saved to get my pilot's license."

"Really?"

"I'll get flying lessons and then get my own plane. I'm done working in any lines. I want the freedom of the sky. You know—the open air."

"It sounds like you are really planning to go." She looked up at him, stretching a bit of cheese that was stringing out from her enchilada to her fork.

"That sounds really great. You've got to take me for a ride in your airplane when you get it. I'd like to fly." She continued.

"I'll take you for a ride as soon as I can. We'll do a trip to the lake and fly low over the water."

"Great," her words trailed off. She looked up at him again and then turned to the waiter, snapping.

"Could you bring another bowl of those chips and some salsa? But mild please, not so hot." She blinked her eyes rapidly, looking up at the waiter.

Turning back to Julio she paused. "I love the chips, but there is too much hot stuff in that salsa. Don't you think? I can't stand the burning."

Julio nodded slowly. He swirled his straw around in his glass and took a long, deep drink. He glanced at the colorful flags moving slowly in the warm air. A wave of familiar melancholy washed over him. Unfortunately, Mary Beth's comments were a deal breaker. This was a first and a last date. Life was much too short to live with someone who didn't like spicy salsa.

BROTHER FOX AND THE DEMOLITION OF THE DEVIL

When Brother Fox said he wasn't getting into the details of the Old Testament because they were nothing but horseshit anyway, we realized there would no longer be any sleeping through Sunday school class. The "we" I'm referring to here were the nine hellion boys my age--well, let's make that 8, because Jeremy Larsen was really more like a girl and he never caused a speck of trouble like the rest of us in the Sterling Second Ward. Bishop Greene must have been pretty desperate or partly off of his rocker to call Blake Fox as the Teacher's Quorum Advisor, that is all I can say. I guess it was the bishop's last resort after we had destroyed four other Sunday school teachers in one year.

Some of these teachers would get angry and call us to repentance; others would lay the guilt on thick as chunky peanut butter on Wonder. Sister Monson just looked at us, blinking slowly, and began to cry like a baby. Three of the four said they hoped their kids never grew up to be like us. I suppose we all considered that a compliment.

In school, Mrs. Walker called our class "the deviants" and threatened us with futures in jail or the garbage disposal business if we didn't straighten up. In church the teachers weren't getting paid, so they just quit when they'd had enough. Brother Fox was different because he had been a deviant like us most his life until he found Jesus.

We all knew about Brother Fox's past. It was a rural legend that grew, inch by inch, like the thistles in the yard or the lift kits on the pickup

38

trucks dragging Main. The Fox name alone was packed with legends: Kenny, Carl, Jamie, Bob—all rebels and tough guys in their own particular way. My old man said when he was younger that even old Bert Fox was hell to reckon with in his shiny '57 Chevy and his hair greased back like the red wave of a flashflood.

The Fox crew made up half of the smokers corner that huddled at lunch hour across from the school property under the old cottonwood trees that pointed their limbs up at the grey winter clouds like skeleton fingers. And if there was an energetic circle of people surrounding a fistfight at the Friday night school dance you could bet your lunch money there would be a Fox involved somehow.

When he was touched by the hand of God, Blake Fox was no different than the rest of his family, driving his GTO straight down the highway to hell. Well, actually, it was the hairpin on the South Hill Canyon Road where Blake Fox didn't make the curve, ended up upside down in a ditch, and nearly met his Maker. I heard he was so wrapped up in the car they had to cut him out with the Jaws of Life. Blake nearly lost his leg and was permanently scarred by a nasty cut above his left eye from some glass. Legend has it that he was hanging in the car for three hours before some farmer pulled off of the road looking for a lost sheep and saw the wreckage. Brother Fox said it was when he lay there entwined in glass and GTO guts that he promised Jesus he'd start going to church and repent of his evil doing.

We were used to hamburger barbecues and Jell-O salad with grated carrots, but the first church outing Brother Fox took us to was the demolition derby at the county fair. Well, it was actually his wife that took us there, because Brother Fox was out in the middle of things in a mean-looking, lime-green Le Baron with Fox's Rock Products spray painted all over it. We all stared at each other and couldn't believe that our teacher was *that* cool. He got hit really hard by the Desert Hardware station wagon in the first round and must have lost his gears, because he rammed his way into second place using only reverse. We hooted and hollered from the bleachers, chucking our popcorn like wild monkeys and howling at the September moon. Sister Fox seemed a bit embarrassed to be there watching her husband and sitting by all of us, but she secretly looked like she approved of it all at the same time.

The Sunday after the demolition derby we talked about crashing it up with Satan.

"It ain't enough to just hit him once, 'cause he'll keep on coming at you until you're broke down and stuck and can't get away," Brother Fox said grinding his fist into his palm. The scar on his forehead would bend at a weird angle a bit when he talked seriously, almost like a question mark, like the scar had a life of its own and was saying, "you got a problem with me, son?"

"Like you, Larry. I seen you hanging out with Brett Derby's boy and I know you probably get into trouble. Right?"

Larry sort of smiled and looked around at all of us.

"Well, you're stupid to hang out with troublemakers like him, looking at Playboys and smoking butts and doing that stuff you think is cool. Ignorant and stupid. Boys," Brother Fox exhaled slowly, blowing the air up his nose, "some of you gotta learn these lessons for yourselves, but I hope some of you can look at my life and see how stupid I've been and not do some of the foolhardy deeds I done. They didn't do me no good. Not one bit." But to us the evil deeds he had done had done him a lot of good. They made him unlike any Sunday school teacher in history, and we all wanted to be just like him.

Most Sunday school lessons you can drift off and be thinking about what football game will be on TV when you get home or if you'll be eating roast beef and potatoes for lunch after church. If, somehow, you get called on to answer a question when you've been dozing and you have no clue about the answer, you are 90 percent safe saying "Jesus." Seriously, He is the answer to the question, nine times out of ten. If it's not "Jesus," than it's "obedience" or "repentance" or "yes" or "no," guaranteed.

With Brother Fox, the answers were different. I mean, he did talk about Jesus and all, but mostly I was awake to know what the questions were. We were kept awake because Brother Fox would mainly not *preach*, but tell us stories from his past. They weren't boring missionary stories from South America about baptizing a line of people in some muddy river or learning to "love the people" either. The stories from Brother Fox were stories about stealing pumpkins at Halloween, racing cars, and cool stuff like that. Usually in the end of the lesson he would toss in a moral statement about why it's not good to do that kind of stuff, or how Jesus wouldn't have approved. Personally, I think he must have been kind-of required to say that stuff at the end of the lesson, because it *was* Sunday school and all.

It was in our third Sunday school lesson that we began planning our first camping trip. You see, it may sound strange, but the Boy Scouts of America and the Sterling Second Ward were basically the same thing— only we wore ties and slacks to one, and green shirts with badges and beads to the other. We planned a trip up the canyon to a mountain lake called Miller's pond to catch some trout and sit around a smoky fire burning hot dogs. We could hardly wait for the day to arrive.

Brother Fox pulled up to the church in his black and white Ford F250, pulling a trailer loaded with four wheelers. There were little ATVs for his kids and bigger ones for us to race around on. His gun rack was loaded with shotguns, too, and he had a long arm clay pigeon thrower mounted in the bed of his pickup. The paint job and pinstripes were new and perfect, and the tailgate was detailed with a fancy calligraphy message, "blew by you." We all loaded our backpacks into his truck and hopped in, screaming our maniacal shouts of a warm Friday night in the prime of our lives.

That afternoon we found a great place to camp. "OK. Bruce, you and Jed got the 12 gauges. Martin and Bob use these 20 gauges. I'll flip the pigeons. Now you boys lineup and we'll play *elimination*. Bob you got first shot. If you miss Martin shoots and if he hits the bird, yer out. If Martin misses then Jed can get you both out. D'ya get it?" Did we get it? We were in ecstasy. Fifteen years old, three feet of deadly steel manliness in our warm live hands—in a *competition*.

The first clay pigeon soared through the air and Bob unloaded both barrels of the 20 gauge in an instant, hitting absolutely nothing. Martin shot too, but he was laughing too hard to even look down the barrel. We all had been shooting cans, rabbits, and birds together with our .22s and BB guns since we were young, but this competitive shooting was different.

41

"Whoa," Brother Fox yelled. "You can't shoot twice, Bob, you little cheating son-of-a-buck. One shot only. And maybe both of you should try aiming next time." He chuckled lowly as he reloaded the pigeon thrower.

Bob was starting to rub his shoulder where the gun had kicked back, looking around slowly to see if any of us were watching.

"Maybe you should reload that sucker," I hinted to Bob from the back of the line.

"Shut up. I was just about to," Bob mumbled. "If you're such a freaking Annie Oakley why don't you come up here in front and show us all how it's done." He stepped back, handing me the shotgun, and Ben Allred pushed me into the front of the line.

"OK. Let me show you women how it's done." I snarled in my best John Wayne drawl.

I loaded two shells into the side-by-side barrels, took a deep breath, and released half of it. The gun felt smooth and heavy in my hands, just like Louis L'Amour described. I looked down the line at my competition and back at the shooting area.

"Pull."

The pigeon arced high over the sagebrush and junipers and I drew the gun up and lead it a little like my dad had taught me. I squeezed slowly on the trigger, not a jerk, and the Day-Glo orange disc exploded.

"Powdered it," cried Brother Fox. "Looks like we got us a competitor here, boys."

Martin was up next. He stopped his giggling and squinted his eyes a little, turning his LA Dodgers hat around backward. He threw the shotgun up to his shoulder aiming out in the brush. Just as he did this, a little cottontail rabbit bounced out from behind a fallen log, and before he even said "pull" Martin squeezed off a shot which echoed off of the cliffs. The rabbit disappeared in a little poof of fur and dust. We were all laughing so hard we almost fell down, but Brother Fox's voiced boomed like a howitzer.

"What the hell was that? Did you just do what I think you did, Mr. Larson?" We all looked around. Brother Fox had never called any of us "Mr." before. "What did that rabbit do to you?"

"Mmm. Nothing," said Martin. "And it never *will* do nothing to me, now," He kidded. Somebody let out half a laugh that stopped as soon as Brother Fox jumped out of the back of the truck.

"Go get it." Brother Fox said calmly.

"What?"

"The rabbit. Go and get it. We're going to clean it and you are going to eat it for dinner. You kill it—you eat it."

"Yeah," said Bob.

"And you're going to help him eat it, Bob." Brother Fox said as he turned Martin's hat back around. We all chuckled. "You're about to find out that rabbit ain't that bad. It actually tastes pretty good, boys. You got to learn; Jesus wouldn't want you out here shooting all of them critters that he made—especially not little cuddly rabbits."

"Right—it tastes *good*. I ain't eating that rabbit," said Martin. "Next thing you're going to tell me is it probably tastes like chicken too, huh?"

"You're fixing to find out tonight, aren't you smart guy." Brother Fox said as he reached in the back of his truck and pulled out a gun that looked like it could shoot small airplanes out of the sky. "You want to show us how manly you are, Martin, give this beauty a try."

"What is that? An elephant gun?" Asked Bob.

"It's a ten gauge—goose gun. Give it a try. You'll have to make sure you keep it real firm against your arm if you don't want a bruise the size of a Twinkie." Brother Fox placed a Coke can out in the sagebrush and returned to us. He wrapped the leather bandolier around his forearm, sighted in, and the gun erupted like Mt. Saint Helens on the poor beverage.

I ran out in the field and set up another can and Martin put the gun up to his shoulder, sweat beading up on his forehead and his hands shaking.

"Hold on," chuckled Brother Fox, as if the gun would take off like a Harley.

Martin fired and the dirt flew up ten feet in front of the can. We all began laughing as Martin spouted off manly phrases like: that was nothing, I barely felt it, and my grandma hits my arm harder than that. He repeated similar manliness around the fire later on, while eating what was left of the cottontail, picking out three shotgun BBs with his teeth. We all ended up trying a taste of the rabbit, which tasted nothing like chicken, in my opinion--more like a burnt, greasy, leather glove.

The next Sunday we had a lesson on bunny rabbits. And sheep. Brother Fox seemed real intent on teaching us a thing or two about respecting God's creations. He even opened up a black leather bound Bible with Blake Fox engraved on the front of it in gold lettering and asked Martin to read aloud to the class.

"Here--read Genesis 1:24. I underlined it," Brother Fox said, passing the Bible over like cinderblock.

Martin read slowly, stuttering through any word over three letters long. "And God made the beast of the earth after his kind and cattle after their kind, and every thing that creepeth upon the earth after his kind: and God saw that it was good."

"See, boys. God made these things, even the creeping things and said they were good. He don't want you killing these good things for the fun of it. And while we're on the subject of animals I found another scripture I think you need to hear. Let's talk about sheep." Brother Fox put his thumbs in his belt and straightened up like a regular preacher. "The Bible is always comparing us people to sheep. I was wondering about that last night so I pondered over a few verses. Let's read this one: John 10:14, in the New Testament. Can you find it? It's on page 134 for you dimwits that don't know what comes after what in the Bible or you don't have those nice tab things to mark your gospels."

Brother Fox pointed an eyebrow at me to read and I cleared my voice and read the verse out loud. "I am the good shepherd, and know my sheep, and am known of mine."

"Now why do you suppose that passage talks about the sheep and the shepherd, boys?" Brother Fox grumbled. "Any of you run sheep up on the mountain? I know Carl's family's got a big herd of cattle. Ben, your family's sheep folks, right?"

"Yep," crowed Ben, sniffing and leaning back on his chair like it was some sort of Lazy-Boy recliner. "My grand-daddy was a sheep man and my dad, too. I don't reckon I'll be continuing the tradition, though. I hate all that shearing and cutting and riding around in the cold weather on some stupid horse."

"Why do you suppose that your sheep need a sheep herder anyway? There ain't any other animals that need herders are there? Carl, you don't have to sit and watch your cows do you? Anybody heard of a chicken herder or a pig herder?" We all began chuckling at the thought of watching chickens all day long.

"It's because sheep are dumb," blurted out Ben leisurely, breaking the silence. "You leave 'em for a few minutes and they get lost, or get caught in a fence, or something. It's like there's always a few really stupid sheep who think they are so smart and they want to go their own way, when they just don't know...you know, they don't know poop from shine-ola. They wander off and then all the sudden it's like—hey, where did all the grass and other sheep go. Oh-oh, here comes a coyote, and then they're dead."

"So what about that scripture? Why do you think that the good Lord compares us to sheep and Himself to the shepherd?" Brother Fox was making sense now. I looked around and I could see everybody was actually alert and paying attention. Even Ben was sitting up in his chair a bit.

"Because we're dumber than hell," I replied.

"Exactly!" Brother Fox pointed at me with the stub of chalk in his fingers. "And watch your mouth in the Lord's house. We all think we know the way to go and we wander around like we got the answers, especially you young bucks—but you're sheep. You're dumb. We need the shepherd, who for all we know hates his job as much as Ben. Poor Jesus, chasing around lost people all the time trying to get them out of fences and keep the coyotes from getting them, or some thieves from eating mutton and sourdough for dinner. Can you boys see what kind of good stories they got in this book?" He was patting his big black Bible gently, like he was burping a newborn baby or something. "I just wish you could read and understand. I sure couldn't when I was your age. Man, it's taken me half of my life just to figure out a few of the 'wherearts' and 'whoa-unto-yuz.' But if you can listen and really hear what this shepherd said, there is some fine stuff, I promise you."

It was on a Friday night Bob and I decided we'd ride our BMX bikes down to the gas station to buy cherry icees and sunflower seeds. It wasn't too late, but it was a Friday and if there was excitement to be had in Sterling, it would be near the gas station. All of the cool high school guys in their pickups would be dragging Main and the Top Stop station was the turn around place on the north end of town, so naturally it was the hot spot and they would always be revving their engines, exiting with a squeal of tires, laying some rubber. People would park their cars, get out and lean on them, and turn up their stereos extra loud so everyone could hear what they were listening to. My mom said I wasn't supposed to hang out at the Top Stop with the high schoolers, or the trouble makers that left high school, yet couldn't leave the high school girls alone. Bob and I would always time our trips for snacks so we could park our bikes, spit seeds, and check out what was happening.

This particular night was a pretty one, with the sun setting in a bonfire on the horizon and a taste of summer in the air. I was racing Bob and bunny hopping the curbs, kicking Coke cans with my back tire and skidding around the corners. When we pulled up to the Top Stop we crashed our bikes out front. We used to have kickstands, but we were past that stage now, so we crashed our bikes whenever we stopped, especially at Top Stop where someone might be watching us.

I was filling up my icee cup to the very top of the clear bubble lid and tamping it with the spoon-straw to settle the air bubbles when I noticed Jamie Fox walk past me. He smelled like smoke and was carrying two cases of Natural Light and a case of Bud to the register. He could barely walk. I couldn't tell if it was because he was drunk, or if it was because he was trying to carry so much beer. I whistled at Bob and we watched as Jamie pulled a wad of money out of his pocket and paid. Nobody messed with Jamie Fox. It was like the guys in the western movies that wear black and silence the bars when they walk in. Bob stepped over and opened the door for Jamie as he walked out.

"Thanks, kid." Jamie snarled and weaved over to a blue Chevy where his friends awaited. I looked out the window as he piled the beer in the back of the truck and jumped up into the cab. Then I stared in shock at the other occupants of the Chevy. The driver was Bob Fox, with his hat turned around backward and a diamond stud earring. Next to him Brother Fox was looking at the front door, where Bob still stood. I couldn't believe it. I blinked my eyes slowly and looked again, hoping I was confused and it wasn't Brother Fox. But it was him, as sure as day. The truck backed up and squealed out of the parking lot.

We rode back to Bob's house slowly, sipping our icees in silence.

Two days later and it was Sunday. We all sat there in the Sunday school room chatting about the week's events and fidgeting with our too-long ties. Bob was discussing Friday night's encounter with Brother Fox with Ben Allred. Ben was talking about how he heard that we should tell the Bishop about that kind of stuff. He said that once his mom saw another church member hitting on his secretary and she went straight to the Bishop. He kept saying it was our duty to help Brother Fox back to the straight and narrow. I had a bitter taste in the back of my mouth listening to him.

I guess I felt betrayed. Or disgusted. I couldn't see how Brother Fox could tell us how we shouldn't be hanging around troublemakers and then he sits in a truck with his cousins as they go to a party somewhere. What kind of example was he setting for us anyway? His lessons didn't make as much sense when you thought of him downing a case of Budweiser while he read his scriptures. I looked at the palms of my hands, breathing in the carpet smell of the church that always seemed to smell new, and decided I would have to have a talk with Brother Fox after church. There was no other way to do it. He had some explaining to do. I think they had a Bible name for his behavior. It was called *hypocrite*.

We waited for ten minutes before the teacher walked into the classroom, and it *wasn't* Brother Fox. Instead of the question mark scar and the pressed pants, we were greeted by jeans, a western shirt with an elk antler bolo tie, and the weathered face of Bob Fox himself. He had taken out his earring, but looked kind of sweaty and uncomfortable. It was the first time any of us had seen him within three blocks of any church and we were immediately silenced. I felt my stomach churn as Bob opened his mouth and said, "Is this the right group of youngsters I'm supposed to be talking with?"

As Bob Fox tried to clear his throat Brother Fox followed him into the class and quietly shut the door.

"I brought my brother in here to help out with the lesson today, boys. I almost had my cousin in here too, but he couldn't quite bring himself to enter the Lord's house. Like I told you, families are important. You gotta stick together." We all stared, our jaws drooping to our knees, as he put his arm around his brother. Then Brother Fox smiled a little bit and turned to Bob. "Actually, why don't we move class outside to the grass and I'll bet we can get Jamie to come over to join us there, too. Peter, why don't you and Little Bob come with me and we'll go out to the truck and talk to Jamie.

I felt a jolt of relief thinking about Brother Fox trying to reunite his family a bit and including us in the process. Bob and I walked with him away from the church and out to an empty spot in the parking lot. Brother Fox was smiling again, staring at the spot where his cousin's truck used to be parked, as he told us we'd have to try to get Jamie next time.

"But don't worry guys, he'll come around. Maybe we should invite him to a camp out first, and work on church later. Either way, we're going to have a good lesson today. My brother Bob's going to help me out. He's got some great stories. You guys are going to like them. Of course I'll throw in a few quotes from the scriptures, too. I really appreciate you guys helping out with my brother. Just go easy on him, he reads a bit slow. He needs you guys as a good influence, a good example. Like you guys are on me. You *know* you teach me more lessons that I ever teach you."

"Really?" I asked, never considering myself an example to anybody. I remembered Sister Monson saying she hoped her kids never grew up like us. Could I really be an example? That was a very scary thought.

"Yep."

We walked over to a shady spot, under a big cottonwood, where the rest of the class was sitting down. I smelled the green in the grass. Summer was on its way; I could feel it warm on my cheeks. Bob sat cross-legged in the shade, plucking blades of grass, but I sat out in the sunlight and closed my eyes.

ALEX PETERSON

JOHN JOHN'S BACKPACK

There is blood on John John's backpack in the bathroom of the McDonalds. He's also got his white socks spotted and resting on top next to a dark smear of fingerprints on his Louis L'Amour novel and his cardboard sign that says he will work for food. John John isn't in the bathroom, and I can't see his legs under the stall. I'm not ready to open it up, so I knock. Nobody.

I somehow go back to eating my hot fudge sundae without enough hot fudge, outside.

Where is he, the owner of the backpack with his name scribbled on it with a blue felt tip marker? Where is John John while his bloody backpack and stuff sits in the McDonald's bathroom on Fifth and State? Is he eating a Big Mac somewhere or looking for his stuff? How can I sit here and eat ice cream while someone is bleeding, without their backpack, in the bathroom of McDonalds? Somehow I manage to do it, like everyone else.

NO WORRIES, MAN

As we walked down the long pier watching the dead, dynamited coral and scattering minnows through the clear water below, we had a plan. It was a plan based on the information in the guidebook and undoubtedly was the same plan that thousands of other young travelers from around the world pursued when they arrived in this same place. Of course we had spoken with others who looked like they were near our budget level by the dirt shoes and on their backpacks, but their replies sound something like this: "Don't plan on staying there for under ten US dollars a night—but the parties there are insane. The raves go on all night." Or, "Laos is where it's at. Like Thailand forty years ago, man."

After a few months of travel advice the words all blend into one big fat blur. Everyone has their own opinions, but at the same time everyone follows basically the same path. They wear the same t-shirts, they want a proper balance of comfort and adventure, but usually lean toward the comfort.

Travel opinions are usually as reliable as the smoking busses, mustached taxi drivers, and creaking boats. And the particular boat ride we had just finished was a Dramamine-induced nightmare lasting three hours longer than it should have, beginning two hours later than it should have. We were rocked and slammed in the massive Indian Ocean swells until I pleaded to Allah or Buddha or Vishnu or Neptune or whatever was out there to please make it calm. Eight hours later, after sacrificing my breakfast and dinner from the night before to the sea Gods, we pulled into the smallish bay of our destination.

The distant view of the bay was beautiful. Actually, it was more than that. The water was the color of Navajo jewelry and the coconut palms littered the beach. However, as we neared the details of the island emerged and the post-card view turned into third-world reality. Our boat hit the jetty and a skinny kid the color of walnut shoe polish with sun bleached hair tied up the poor wooden vessel. We knew we had at least one week on the island before the boat would come back again.

As we stepped off of the long pier onto the island I realized that our plan was a stupid one. We were in a group of tiny islands, small enough to walk around in a few hours, and we had planned on walking across the island we were currently on, to the huts on the more remote side. We chose this island because the Lonely Planet didn't write much about it, which typically meant it would be quiet and deserted. The LP map was easy to read and the distance looked very walkable. Then, I looked across the bay at another island, the one that everyone (as well as the book) had recommended, and realized the boat ride across the channel would be even shorter than walking to the other side of the island we were on. Upon further inspection, the island we were now standing on looked like a dump, coated with a ragged layer of garbage and half-burned coconut husks.

The Indonesian sun seared down on us from high above. I licked my lips and made a conscious effort to think clearly, even if my inner dialog involved substantial turmoil.

"Ah, the adventure of new places; the excitement of the unknown," I thought, "The life blood of the traveler and the headache entwined in one.

"Mosquitoes. Malaria."

"Think Lewis and Clark, Darwin, Paul Theroux. Think Huck Finn down the river."

"Damn it is hot. Can it really be this hot?"

" 'Books are fine in their own right, but they are a mighty bloodless substitute for life.' Who was that? Robert Louis Stevenson?"

"Didn't he die of Tuberculosis?"

I stepped into the only shade around, next to a broken lean-to assemblage. Indecision. Just what I didn't need. I verbalized it.

"What do you think about that other island, Monica?" I asked.

She glared at me and a drop of sweat rolled off of her nose onto the blazing sand under her feet. Her eyes spoke more clearly than any moving tongue. "I *thought* that we had decided. Let's stay at the place we looked at in the book. I am hungry. I don't want to think about it," they said.

Those hazel eyes had every right to be grumbling—there was some sort of a nightmarish math equation for it. Take the uneasy feeling of arriving in a new and dangerous place, multiply that by some churning sea sickness and blazing heat, add a lack of lunch. Finally, divide the sum with the musical score from the boatman's stereo (his only tape was Bryan Adams' smash hits)--you've got the formula for disaster. $D=BA$ or something. You know it's true. Everything I do, I do it for you.

"Well, now that other island looks closer. We have to walk all the way to the other side of *this* island," I replied. "Plus, this place looks thrashed. Look at it." I slowly moved my arm in a broad sweep like an ugly and unshaven Vanna White displaying a shiny new car. A small lizard ran across an old diaper on the ground, making a noise like a rattlesnake. I spat at it.

"Forget it. We're staying here." I wished her cold tone could somehow condition the air.

"Let me go get some Cokes." I reached into my pocket for coins and looked over to see if the little shack next door had anything drinkable.

As I turned around, I ran straight into a dark little monster of a man wearing a worn out straw hat that resembled a flattened tumbleweed on his huge head. His pock marked face gave way to a sly smile, and he commenced to scratch his temple with a stubby finger. He looked different than the surrounding locals, darker, maybe Melanesian? The guy moved slowly and deliberately and his hair was tight and curly, tucked under his hat.

"Hey, Dude, you gotta place to stay?" He looked up at me with bulging eyes. Eyes like ping pong balls. I remembered the advice of an experienced backpacker. He told me, while traveling, always know where you are going. If you don't actually know where you are going, which is often the case, then learn to fake it. Never, absolutely never, open up a Lonely Planet book in an airport or bus stop and look for a place to stay. Read up before you get there, when there aren't quick, famished eyes looking for your rupiah, baht, dollars, or whatever else you might be packing in your money belt or that little bag dangling around your neck with your passport and credit card in it.

From the man's short statement I realized three essential things: number one--Monica and I had been talking too loudly; number two--our bumbled plan was an obvious wreck and this man knew we needed a place to stay; and number three--this man was not to be trusted at any expense--because of the Dude Factor.

The Dude Factor, or DF, states that anyone who you first meet and addresses you in the "dude" form should never be trusted. No, more than that--these people should be fled from immediately. No matter what country you are in, or whether the communication is over the phone or live conversation, the DF indicates that the person is trying to be too friendly too fast, and obviously wants to rip you off.

"No, we've got a place already. Thanks," I replied.

"Where you from, man? England?" His accent was thick, but his English was understandable and he had some slang down-- must have learned it from traveling surfers. "Australia, mate? No. Canada. That is it."

He thought I was Canadian. Did I say "a-boot?" "Get oat of here?" I didn't think so. And I wasn't sporting a maple leaf flag patch on my backpack like every other Canadian, trying to distinguish themselves from their imperialist southern neighbors.

"We're from the United States."

"American, huh? We don't see many of your people here," he took off his hat, fanning himself, and his jack-in-the-box Afro must have heard my patriotic acknowledgement because it exploded like a Fourth of July firework. "From New York or Chicago?"

"Edmonton."

"Oh yes. Near California?"

"Something like that." I looked over at him and smiled a quick smile. The little man returned the toothy demonstration by producing exquisitely white choppers of his own. He asked where we were going.

"We are going to the Blue Coral Bungalow. On the other side." This was our plan, even though we had no clue what the place was like. That side of the island wasn't really described in the travel book, which was our main reason for choosing it.

"There isn't anyone there. It's empty. I'll show you a better place. My place."

So he was a hit man: a guy looking for a commission from the hotels for dragging tourists in from the boat launch. I should have figured. Or maybe he simply wanted to take us into the jungle and steal our backpacks like the guidebooks and travel legends warned us about.

"No, really. We want to walk over by the Blue Coral. We like that side," I tried not to stutter.

"What do you mean? You have never been here."

"How do you know?"

"Because if you stayed at the Blue Coral you wouldn't go back," he laughed. "My place is better. But no pressure, though. Take you time. Come check out my place. No worries." He walked away slowly toward the shade of a palm down the white trial. There were no roads on the island, only trails for small wooden carts pulled by sweating ponies. The man effortlessly walked barefoot over the crushed coral paths, which were ripping apart my sandals. He leaned up against the tree and gazed out at the ocean, giving up on us too easily.

I purchased a bottle of Coke and another of water and returned to

Monica.

She took a long, slow drink and spoke up. "Let's just find a place to get rid of these backpacks and relax. I just don't want to get on another boat today. I'm done with them. Let's stay here tonight, even if it is a dump." She was right. No more boats. My stomach churned with the thought of a rolling horizon, motor exhaust, and D=BA .

"OK. Let's walk to the Blue Coral."

"That was the original plan," she mumbled as she finished off her water.

We began trudging down the trail, watching the breakers crash out on the reef, and feeling our shirts soaking up the sweat.

The first bungalow we came upon looked like it had just been destroyed by a hurricane or typhoon or cyclone or whatever they called those big storms in this part of the world. The stick structures were falling and dilapidated, the roofs caved in, and several crumbling cement ruins lay barren in front with no visible purpose.

"Nice place," Monica commented sarcastically as we walked by.

The next two bungalows were a little better looking, but were also empty. The beach was pristine, long and white, but there were no people. No tourists, no locals--nobody. It was strange. A few scrawny cows roamed through the ruins, banging the old bells around their slim black necks like bovine cathedrals, while they scavenged for something green to eat.

We could hear a pony drawn carriage coming up the trail behind us, so we stepped onto the sandy shoulder of the path to let them by. But, instead of passing, the cart stopped and the man next to the driver jumped down into the sand.

"Come on. I'll take you to my place. No worries." It was the same small man with the tumbleweed hat. He had followed us. "My friend here will give you a ride to the bungalow. It's very hot to walk."

"We like the exercise," I responded. "We've been sitting on a boat all day."

"OK." He mumbled something in Indonesian to the cart driver, who turned the pony around and sped off in a cloud of dust. "I'll walk with you. My name is Martin. My place is close. You will really like it. But if you don't, no worries, just go to the other place. But you are going to like it, for sure, man."

Though I didn't trust this man for a minute, I had to admire his persistence. He waddled off toward a group of palm trees in the distance and we shrugged our shoulders and followed him.

"No worries?" I mumbled.

He guided us away from the beach path and we began to walk inland, passing a smelly cesspool of mud. Each footstep left a little poof of white dust as we dodged liquidy green dribbles of cow shit and leaned away from thorny shrubs next to the path.

"Where are we going?" I finally asked, getting weary of becoming a statistic or a scary travel legend of why not to follow strangers. Monica glanced at me uncertainly.

"It's right here. See the huts?" Martin pointed up the path. I could see five thatched roofed cottages and one large structure with large wooden crossbeams and a huge yellow, red, green, and black flag. As we walked closer I could see the flag had a silhouette of Robert Nesta Marley and several giant ganja buds adorning its center. "See. I told you it is so nice here. I run this place with my friend from France. Take a look at this room. It is the only one left." He motioned us to the closest of the huts.

We dropped our backpacks in the shade of the porch and walked into the nicest bungalows we had seen in months. The ceilings were high and made of tightly woven thatched fronds. The floors were blue and white tiles and the bed was large and new, covered in clean white sheets. There was a huge skylight window above, which gave a spectacular view of the towering volcanoes on Lombok (and later we would watch the Southern

Cross at night). The furniture was thick, well crafted bamboo. A beautiful lace mosquito net dangled over the bed. The bathroom was outside, open to the flowers of the jungle, and lined with walls mortared with round stones and shells from the beach. We were in shock. The place would have been fantastic if we were expecting it, but the surprise made things even better.

"No worries man. If you want to eat lunch and think about it my wife will cook you some mee goreng. She is the best cook on the island, I say."

"OK. How much for the room?" I knew something was too good to be true.

"Nine dollars per night for the two of you. The price is high because we have fresh water in the shower. We're the only place on this side of the island. We bring it here on a ship from Lombok," Martin said quickly.

"Really? No fresh water?" I couldn't believe it.

"There is only salt water here. Ask anyone. I like to wash off after I swim in the salt, and so does Louis. It was his idea to bring water in the boat. The rainwater gets used too fast."

We sat down for lunch on huge red cushions around a low bamboo table listening to French hip-hop that boomed bass from the massive sound system hanging from the rafters. Martin brought out two fragrant portions of mee goring on banana leaf plates and placed them in front of us.

"Bon appetite, man. Tell me if you have ever tasted better food. My wife is a great cook, I'm telling you."

We ate every noodle and piece of cabbage, licking the banana leaf clean afterward. It was simple and delicious.

"Let's stay here tonight and check out the Blue Coral this afternoon. But I have a feeling that we will want to stay here a while," Monica said sleepily, her belly bulging, but not as much as mine.

"Good idea," I turned my sagging eyes toward the kitchen. "Martin. Give us the room for eight dollars and we will stay."

"Eight fifty. Eight if you stay two nights or more."

"Deal."

"Great. You will like it here. No worries, man." Martin folded his arms. "Go rest for a while. Later I will show you magic. Do you like magic? I am a great card trick man. I know 108 tricks. I have the skills of magic from my grandfather in Timor. That's where I am from." He held up a well-worn pack of damp playing cards and began to flip them into piles on the table.

"Choose three cards. Don't show me," he said smoothly. Monica grabbed three different ones and put them back into the pile. "Is this one?"

"No."

"Of course it is not. I'm kidding with you." Martin then flipped the cards quickly through his fingers with incredible dexterity, pulling out three cards and rolling them keenly over his knuckles. "These are your cards for real. Right?"

Monica examined them slowly, the sedation of the big meal slowing her vision. "Yes. They are. How did you do it?"

"I can't tell you. I'm magic. I told you." His eyes bulged a bit more than their normal bulging. "Tomorrow I'll tell you your father's name by magic and it will make you crazy with curiosity because I'm magic."

We all blinked slowly and breathed in the ocean breeze. "OK, then. Tomorrow." We rolled ourselves off the cloudlike cushions that didn't even smell like mildew yet.

"Go rest. No worries, man."

The next morning was fresh, the sun rising over the ocean quickly into a cloudless sky. I arose early, put on my running shoes, which felt strange and itchy after wearing only flip-flops for a month, and ran along the beach. I ran until I came back to where I started, a complete orbit of the entire island in forty minutes. It was smaller than I had imagined and shaped like a big sandy turtle poking its back out of the blue-green water. Before I walked back to the bungalow I swam out into the clear water, opening my eyes beneath the surface to watch the blurring colors of brilliant fish in the coral.

When I got back to the room Monica was sitting on the bamboo couch on the porch, a clear cup of steaming tea in her hands.

"Bonjourno," I surprised her. "How did you sleep?" I felt the edgy travel anxiety washed away by the run and swim, and I hoped Monica was feeling relaxed too.

"I had some strange dreams," she said, sipping her tea. "It was probably from that fish last night. Fish always gives me weird dreams. I dreamt that Martin was doing some card tricks and he called his son to bring him a drink of water. This little boy emerged from the back room, a cute little barefoot kid, maybe ten or eleven. When the kid set down the glass I smiled at him. He smiled back--a big toothy grin. That is when I saw his teeth. It was terrible. They looked like shark teeth, Al, sharp and triangular. Then the kid turned into this monster and I ran away."

"Strange," I said, bending over to stretch my legs and back. She sipped her tea quietly. "It must have been the fish dreams. But it's a beautiful day today. Do you want to go snorkeling? I want to check out the ocean trench and the sea wall and look for turtles. Martin said he would take us in his friend's boat."

"Sounds good. Let's go get some breakfast first," she suggested, rubbing her belly. "No more fish for a while."

We ate banana pancakes and Martin brought them out with another plate of fresh pineapple, papaya, and bananas. We ate slowly and talked with our new acquaintance as he cleaned the long fingernail on his pinkie with a penknife.

"Do you have any family on the island Martin?"

"Only my wife's family. I'm not from this place. I'm from Timor, to the east. I am not like these people. My family is all in Timor, far away. But the tourism there is bad now, and the Muslims killed many of the

Christians. Terrible times. My uncle and aunt were shot by the army—for nothing. I left and my French friend needed someone who spoke Indonesian. Here I am."

"How long have you been here?" Monica questioned.

"Five years now. I like the traveling people I meet, but the islanders are quite unfriendly. I am not Muslim, you see. Everyone thinks I am, but I am not. I had to convert to Islam to marry my wife, get property papers, and make my wife's mother happy--how do you say it? Mother of law? But I won't bow down and pray five times a day like my wife. I'm really a Christian, dude. And I fool them."

"That sounds like a mess," I commented.

"No worries man. I'm cool with it," he smiled, scratching his belly over his worn out T-shirt. "Well, you want to go snorkeling and see giant clams? Also we can go to lunch on the other island and I will show you the big cannons there in the hill that the Japanese built to fight the Americans during the war. And maybe we'll see some papayas," Martin winked at me and walked toward the ocean.

We spent the morning swim drifting in the strong currents, looking down 50 feet through the crystal water at slowly swimming sea turtles with velvety backs. The boat would drop us at the edge of the sea wall and we would cruise like human torpedoes in the ten mile-per-hour current to the opposite end of the wall. The deep trench was dark near the bottom, but we could watch the fish, some of them groupers with gaping mouths and looked like they could swallow small dogs. The spotted fish would poke their heads out of their nooks and caves, gazing up at us with curious eyes, opening and closing their lips like congested children at the dinner table.

Upon arrival at the boat Martin would ask us to describe the fish we saw and then he would identify them, point his stubby finger at their pictures in a small, water-stained, French book. He was terrified of the open water, but he loved to look at the sea creatures by dangling his masked face over the edge of the boat.

"It's great. Really. You should have seen it five years ago before dynamite fishing. Much better. You want to float it again? No worries man."

We snorkeled the entire morning and decided to motor over to another island for a late lunch at Martin's suggestion. Leaning back on the outboard motor we moved slowly across the calm bay and Martin began to talk.

"It's too crowded with Europeans and loud for me over there. I like it more quiet. But they have good lunch. And good papayas." He winked at me again and whispered in my ear. (Papayas are what I call the women who lie on the beach with no shirts on. They like that in Europe.) Speaking up Martin continued, "I think the naked people are very disrespectful here. The Muslims even cover their heads and these European women show their bodies." He paused, exhaling. "It is a shame." (Oh well, let's go look, he whispered).

We dropped a pretzel shaped rebar anchor just off of the beach of the big island and waded in to a small restaurant for rice and fish. The road along the beach was sprinkled with bungalows and tourist trinket shops selling batik sarongs, T-shirts, and little shell sculptures. There were old water bottles and garbage strewn haphazardly along the beach and road and there weren't many people in sight. The island was not as nice as the island we were staying on. The town looked like a place where the party was over and nobody wanted to clean up.

We happily and hungrily consumed fried rice with two small whole fish served on the same style of biodegradable, banana leaf plates.

"Come on. I will show you around town," said Martin, picking the fish out of his teeth with a small stick. As we walked down the beach a few hundred meters we discovered where all of the tourists were. The waves gently lapped the coral white sand that was littered with lounging bodies. A few people swam in the gentle surf, a group of sweating tattooed fellows kicked around a flat soccer ball, and a half a dozen women lay in the sand tanning everything that wasn't covered by their bikini bottoms.

We walked past the beach and back to our little outrigger boat bobbing in the waves. Martin winked at me again as we adjusted ourselves on the hot wooden seats and he pulled the starter on the motor.

"The papayas are small this year," he chuckled along with the idling motor.

After a day of snorkeling we decided to explore the island for a day by circling around the beach and returning through the coconut farms on the main trail. The beach was easy to walk on at low tide, the sand squeaking with glee at each footstep. Little red crabs with blue legs scurried about the beach, hiding in their holes as we walked by and then jumped out again to continue their business of making strange, spiraling asymmetric designs with little balls of sand.

We collected long conical shells and round skeletons of sea urchins, placing them in piles near the high tide mark for our little Indonesian pineapple girl friends. The little girls were all business when we first met them, their faces sternly mimicking their parents and the local storeowners.

"I make good price for you, Mister," said one little girl, pushing her hair back out of her eyes. "Give me 5,000 for delicious pineapple."

"No, buy from me Mister," squealed her taller friend, trying to look mean. She couldn't have been more than twelve. "My pineapple better." They commenced with their yelling at each other in Indonesian, giving hand motions like you would to a dog to make it go away. The youngest of the three girls sat back under the shade of a coconut palm, picking her fingernails with her kitchen knife, just trying to stay out of the competition.

"I'll pay 4,000," I finally said looking at each girl, putting on my own bargaining face.

"No Mister. You pay 5,000," the older girl said. I began to walk away and they both yelled "OK, 4,000!" I smiled and bought one from each girl. Monica then bought a pineapple from the youngest girl in the shade to make it even. As the girls sat down and began peeling and diagonally cutting out the dark spines with their old rusting kitchen knives the girls lost their business faces and became little girls again. They laughed loudly and threw pineapple skins at each other. Their broken English and our terrible Bahasa Indonesian combined for some interesting conversations that usually ended up with everyone running out into the ocean or a surprise attack, wet-sand fight.

The girls followed us around the island, giggling and occasionally attempting to sell pineapple to the scattered European tourists. When we arrived back at our bungalow the girls shied away and asked us if this was really where we were staying.

We told them yes and that it was quite nice, and invited them in for a soda.

"The man who works there is a bad man. We won't go near him," the girls looked in the direction of our room in horror.

"What?" I asked.

"He is not good."

"Bad."

"He is evil. Vedy vedy bad. We cannot tell you why. Be careful." The girls backed away down the trail to the beach, never turning their backs toward the bungalow. As I looked closer they each had their rusty kitchen knives held in their hands underneath their dirty pineapple baskets.

"How strange," Monica commented.

"Yeah. Martin said he didn't quite fit in here, but those girls were spooked. Superstitious, I guess. Weird. Maybe it's because he's not a good Muslim?" I shook the sweat off of my head like a dog. "I'm going swimming before I cook myself. Last one to the beach is a rotten pineapple," I shouted already taking a head start down the sandy trail.

Monica turned the other way and yelled, "You go. I'm going to shower and wash off this salt."

I swam outside the shore break and floated high in the cool water in a fleshy X, letting the small ripples make muffled music in my ears.

As I returned to the bungalow I could tell something was wrong. Monica sat on the bed looking at the wall with a blurred look in her eyes.

"Someone was spying on me in the shower, Al," she said calmly.

"What? Are you sure? Who was it?" I said in shock.

"I don't know. I was washing the shampoo out of my eyes and I looked out through the crack in the rocks and there were two eyes staring back at me." She sniffed. "I said 'hey' and they disappeared. I stepped up on the toilet and looked over the wall into the jungle but I couldn't see or hear anybody. It kind of freaked me out, though. I don't know how long the guy was there."

"Who did it look like?"

"I don't know. It was just eyes and I had shampoo in *mine*."

"I'll go tell Martin. Or do you think it *was* Martin?"

"I don't know, Al."

"Well, I will go look out there and see if anyone is still there. OK?" I said as I walked around the side of the bungalow and into the wall of thick leaves and undergrowth outside. I searched everywhere around the bungalow, but found no clue of a person. I decided not to tell Martin about it, suspecting he might be the culprit.

Later, as we sat back in the hammocks of the restaurant Martin switched the CD to some techno music with wild jungle animal screams and African chants sampled into a heavy drum and bass.

"You ready for a card trick, man?" He said slowly swinging my hammock with his hand.

"Sure. What have you got?" I dog-eared the page I had sleepily repeated twice already.

Martin pulled up a small table and began shuffling the deck. "Which trick you want? Seven to three? Four eyed tiger? Lucky nines? What?"

"Show me a difficult one," I asked, scratching a mosquito bite on my shoulder and feeling the crisscross indentations of the hammock on my back. He squatted by the table, shuffling.

"OK. Choose four cards and don't tell me."

Martin completed his card trick and once again amazed me with his talent and dexterity. I was completely stumped with his moves. I had seen a friend in college perform tricks, but Martin good—really good.

"Tell me a clue about how you do it." I prodded. He shuffled again and said, "OK. A clue. Usually I don't tell my secrets, but these tricks aren't magic. These are skill tricks. The magic tricks rely on my power. With these tricks I concentrate on which cards have been placed, in my head, and the cards that aren't there are the ones you choose. It's mathematics, man."

"You really counted the cards and knew which were missing?"

"Yeah." He repeated the trick again. I was completely baffled. This was very impressive. "Let me show you another one," he paused, "in just a minute. Here comes someone and I have to fill one of the bungalows."

Martin jogged down the trail toward the beach and returned five minutes later lugging a large, new backpack with an Asian-looking traveler behind him, then another Asian girl. "Japanese," I thought to myself.

Martin showed them the bungalow and jogged back to the card table with a grin exploding across his pockmarked face.

"Wow. They took it. Don't tell anyone, but they are paying $40 US per night for this place." Martin was looking mischievous, his eyebrows raised and his wrist wiping the perspiration from his forehead and pushing back his flopping hair. "I just said ko-ni-chi-wa and bowed and they came right in. Those Japanese always fall for that. Pretend you're Japanese or know their ways and they trust you."

"That is a lot of money."

"I don't think so. They don't think so. It's a small price after what they did to my grandmother on Timor during World War Two. My grandfather would kill them today if he were here. A kill stroke," he held my shoulder with one hand, held his hand out like a stubby sword with the other, and swiped the pinkie side of the sword across my throat.

I swallowed. Loudly. His voice was smooth and quiet now and Martin was sweating like a cold Coke bottle.

"During the war," he continued, the Japanese soldiers killed most of the men and forced the women to sleep with the officers of the army. My grandmother was a whore for the Japanese and became pregnant. When my grandfather came out of the jungle and found out, he killed the baby. He still will kill Japanese if he sees them. They were very bad to my people." Martin nodded at the cabin. "I am not so angry. I only take their money to make them pay for their behavior. They killed many people. Not just Muslims, but good Christians."

I didn't quite know what to say. "Yeah, that is the hell of war, I guess. But these (I pointed) people here didn't rape your grandmother. Neither did their parents." I risked playing the Devil's advocate.

Martin turned, his eyes angry and his forehead a leaking faucet.

"Their people are the same. They deserve the kill stroke." He slowly moved his fleshy sword of an arm across the hot air in front of him, one eye closed, his thick hair tilted to one side. "But for now I just take their money. Ari-gato. You want another trick of the cards?" He then laughed and smiled, but with a strange look in his bugging eyes.

"Ah, no thanks. I'm going for a swim. Maybe later," I said, closing up my book and strolling toward the beach, remembering to lock my door and bolt it from the inside at night. At least the Americans were fighting the Japanese during the war and not the Indonesians.

The next week seemed to pass by like a time elapsed film shot. I would wake up at sunrise for a journey around the island, watching the sun blast into the honey orange sky while the distant volcanoes in Bali and Lombok watched over us like protective mothers. Monica and I spent our time imitating our beloved sea turtle friends. We floated around the island, relaxed on the cotton-white sand, and ate half of our body weight in fresh fish. Each of us finished several books and we became fairly good friends with Martin--witnessing the majority of his 108 card tricks.

The weekly boat returned to the island to drop off fresh tourists and take back brown ones and we found ourselves deciding to spend our last week in similar turtle fashion. We figured we would simply take the next weekly boat back to Bali the day before our flight home. Or maybe we would stay until we got old.

Later that day the Germans arrived. They were not satisfied with their previous hotel because of a toilet that ran continuously, evening mosquitoes, and a "constant mold smell." I knew this because the German girl would not stop complaining about the place for a solid hour while we ate pineapple pancakes next to them for breakfast.

The German guy had many similar complaints: the conservative Muslim attitude, the country politics, the lack of sanitation, and the fact that the only vegetable on the island was cabbage. I supposed they were venting, but once it started they would take turns and the irritating feeling would build like scratching the mosquito bites behind your knees.

"Zhis place will have to do until zhe ship comes again to take us back to semi-civilization," the girl snarled.

Our attempts to change the subject weren't working, and Monica was starting to get annoyed. "You are in the freaking tropics in a third world country dear," Monica's eyes said to me as she nodded. "There are mosquitoes, strange smells, and mold here. Deal with it." Finally the German girl spoke about something else.

"How much you pay for zhis place?" she asked, her nostrils flaring as she squinted her eyes behind her futuristic uber-thin glasses.

I told her and she chuckled something in German to her companion.

"We pay less than you. You have to bargain to make the price lower. These Indonesians will take all of your money."

We nodded. "True, but we don't care so much. This place is nice and mellow and the food is pretty good," I said and shrugged. Apparently Monica and I hadn't realized that things were so bad on the island.

"Did you see the fish yet?" The guy asked.

"Yeah. We eat them every night," Monica smiled, rubbing her tanned belly.

"No. The ones in the sea."

"Yeah. Those are nice too. The sea wall has a fun current to drift in and there are all sorts of fish there. Martin can hook you up with a boat," Monica was still rubbing her belly.

"I do not really like zhat man. We will not go with him. We can swim ourselves," the girl was flaring her nostrils again.

"Whatever you want. The fish are nice from the shore, too. But there are a lot of turtles near the sea wall." I replied.

Needless to say, we ran into the German couple a lot during the next week on the tiny island. We even ended up eating together a few times just to have someone to chat with.

That night we ate dinner at sunset on the beach, the small wooden tables lit up warmly with candles placed in cut off plastic water bottles filled with sand to keep them from blowing out. We had four choices of fish, which were each brought to the table in a large aluminum tub for us to select our victim to eat.

It was pleasant to chat with others about traveling to far off places. The Germans had traveled only through parts of Europe, but they had high hopes of seeing the far off edges of the planet in their high-top hiking boots and dark wool socks, which they only took off only to sleep or swim. Klaus and Sabrina spoke of Egypt and India in the future. Indonesia was their experimental third world country; a gauge of their stamina and interest in future exotic travel in places with a lot more dirt and dysentery. They spoke of their past travel experiences in hip bars and cheap hotels in Prague, sun-bleached beaches in Greece, and a house in Spanish wine country. The sky slowly smoldered on the horizon and gradually faded through ten shades of pastels into the dark of the sea.

After dinner we decided to relax on the huge pillows at our bungalow restaurant. We buzzed to a fine blend of acid jazz and reggae as the moon danced into the sky. After a while Martin showed up with his son carrying a small puppy.

"How's it going? Guten tag?" he asked, drumming a rhythm on the bar.

"Very chill. Listening to music here. What's up, Martin?" replied Monica, reclining back on a huge purple pillow. The Germans nodded slowly at Martin.

"Come and show us some more card tricks before you disappear and fly away to Las Vegas," I added.

"OK. OK. You ready for my best trick? Let me tell you your father's name. I am feeling the magic power tonight."

"Right on," I looked up at the palm-thatched roof at a nearly translucent, ghost-white gecko eating mosquitoes above the dangling light bulb. Martin settled down next to us on the smooth hardwood floor and I moved my little blue cloud over to make room. The Germans chatted to each other quietly and eyed Martin. The dark little man sat perfectly erect, cross legged, like an Afro topped monk, his wide pink bottomed feet in his hands as he breathed deeply—in through his nose, out through his mouth. We all watched his preparations, trying to conceal the grins that nearly erupted in contagious spasms.

"OK," Martin exhaled. "Write your father's name down on this little piece of paper and then roll it up into a tight ball."

"Whoa. Wait a minute here," Monica exclaimed. "You said you could guess it."

"I only need this one to warm up," he replied as he itched his billowing fro and closed his dark, bugging eyes.

I complied and placed the tiny paper ball on the low bamboo table between us. Martin slowly touched the ball three times, his eyes half open now. As he lifted his hands over the paper it began to levitate off of the table. We all gasped.

"Whoa!" Klaus and I exhaled. I blinked again in the dim light, feeling the Bintang beer tingle behind my eyelids.

"This is fake." Sabrina was watching closely and she leaned toward the table. She reached her finger out and touched the air above the little ball. The ball jerked sideways and Martin's eyes opened wide.

"I told you this is a warm up. Don't meddle in the process."

"He's lifting it with a hair tied to zhe paper," yelled Klaus, deafening my left ear with his thick accented Bintang breath.

"Oh. I see it," said Monica, smiling, and readjusting her butt in the pillow.

"Your father is Larry, right?" Martin asked.

I nodded slowly. "Yes, it sure is. I didn't even see you read it. That was pretty good," I mumbled.

"That was not pretty good. That was not even magic. I'm only warming up. Now we do it for real," Martin coughed, momentarily producing the look of a Maori warrior's face just before he smashes the European sailor's head with a bone studded battle club. We all leaned backward and looked slowly at each other. The relaxed atmosphere was completely gone. Martin commenced to crack each knuckle loudly and whispered for Sabrina to sit next to him.

"I'll tell you your father's name without the paper now. But this is serious magic. You need to be quiet."

We all crouched closer now as Martin repeated his meditation and blinked his eyes rapidly. The geckos on the ceiling made some strange chirping noises and looked down with bubbly black eyes. The jungle frogs and insects seemed to get very quite, like a giant, omnipotent finger was turning down the volume. The trance song on the stereo faded out and died. The CD player shuffled to the next disc. The eerie feeling crept between us all and we looked around at each other as Martin hummed a low note in the back of his throat.

The stereo buzzed and the next song began with an offbeat muted guitar—da-dee-deet, da-dee-deet, dee-deet. It was the beginning of *Get Up Stand Up*. Monica giggled. I looked around.

"This is stoopid," Klaus moaned.

Martin's eyes opened wide, his fro vibrating. The Maori warrior face reappeared. He looked around at each of us and I felt a smirk coming on, but also gratitude that I wasn't Captain Cook.

"You do not believe me?" said the warrior face. Look at the little ball of paper."

Sabrina opened the little wad in anticipation. She stared hard through her stylishly small wire glasses and blinked slowly, her mouth slightly ajar. She blinked, wrinkled up her nose, and relaxed it again.

"This must be fake. Klaus, did you tell him my father's name? He can't know." We all looked at the little white piece of paper in her hand.

"I told you I am magic. Now you feel my power." Martin spun around on his back like a break dancer, stepped down onto the dirt, and walked off into the jungle, his son and the puppy slowly trailing behind him. On the little paper were the names of each one of our fathers.

"Do you want me to buy your boat ticket to return to Bali?" Martin asked as we ate breakfast next to the Germans. "I'll pick up the tickets on the other side of the island today, no worries. You don't have to pay me. I'm going anyway."

I looked at Monica, raising my sun-bleached eyebrows. The Germans quietly grunted at each other with throaty verbs.

"Sure," Monica said, nodding, and swirling around the last of her tea in the clear glass cup. "Here is some money."

"No thank you. We will go," Klaus groaned, looking at the table and tapping his fingertips on the batik tablecloth.

"OK. No worries. I'll be back."

I handed Martin a small wad of rupiahs for the ticket and he walked away through the jungle, his dark body disappearing quickly like camouflage.

"Well, we are going snorkeling today. What are your plans?" Monica asked Sabrina.

"I'm so tired of this place. I don't know what to do. I'm bored of the water and the sun. Maybe I'll go back to bed," grumbled Sabrina. "I just need a change. I'm ready to be back home and drink a good cup of coffee in the cool air."

"Yeah. I'm ready to read the newspaper. Traveling is exciting for a while, but it starts to seem the same. I'm ready for my own bed and a vegetable other than cabbage," said Klaus.

"I know what you mean," I spoke up. "There comes a time when your drifting, comes a time when you settle down. Neil Young said that once. I say that sometimes you just need to go home." I didn't feel like my time had come yet, but it was obvious that our friends were ready to leave. I yawned as the Germans walked back to their room.

"Hey look, there is Martin's son," Monica pointed behind the kitchen where a young boy in a shredded swimsuit shyly poked his head around the corner. She got up and walked back to the kitchen and whispered *selemat pagi* to the giggling kid. Monica held out her hand and the child approached like a wild monkey after a mango. Very slowly the boy held hands with Monica and peeked out to take a closer look at us.

"Apa ka nama awat?" Monica asked. The boy smiled when she asked his name, revealing pointed, shark-like teeth.

"Did you see that?" I mumbled.

"Just like my dream, Al. Freaky."

"Strange. I think I recall something about this ritual of sharpening children's teeth with a file to make them look scary—to ward off evil spirits or something. I thought the practice was banned now in Indonesia, but maybe it's not."

"Frankie," whispered the ghost child. "Nama saya Frankie."

"Hello, Frankie," Monica whispered back and I reached out my hand above his head, beckoning a high five. The young boy jumped up and slapped my hand, which produced a huge smile and several grunts. His teeth gave the poor kid a terrifying look. They couldn't make him very popular with the other kids on the island. It was obvious from his reaction to any human contact that he was usually isolated or ostracized by his peers. Or maybe the other kids were just scared of him.

Monica motioned to Frankie to come to the beach with us. We started walking toward the ocean, the small boy following timidly behind us. Monica and I looked at each other in pleasant surprise, then looked back to see the kid. He was gone. The undergrowth near the trail still wiggled slowly where Frankie jumped into the dark refuge of the jungle. We continued on slowly toward the sound of the breakers on the coral sand.

"Didn't that freak you out? How could you do that to a kid?" Monica asked.

"Yeah. But maybe it's just a cultural thing we don't understand. I don't know. Like pierced ears."

"But I had a dream of that kid with his teeth." The wind was blowing gently onshore. We continued walking down the beach.

"I admit it is weird. But it was only a dream."

"Maybe you're right. But it's still freaking me out."

"We have to go tomorrow. If we don't then we will miss the plane in Bali," I said as Monica rolled over in the sand, making a human corndog out of herself.

"But I don't want to leave," she moaned in a strong British accent, a wave gently rolling us over. She held her pineapple on a stick high in the air like an Olympic torch.

"Mister!" cried a girl in a weathered halter top and cut-off shorts from the shade of a coconut tree. It was the shy girl from before. "Buy pineapple from me, Mister!" She smiled a gorgeous little smile and held out three fingers—the price. I gave her the thumbs up and turned to Monica, who was beginning to look like the dark skinned local children from lounging in the sand in her bikini for the last few weeks.

"I'd like to stay too, but we can't miss our plane. The Germans have a flight the same day as us. We can travel back to Bali with them and share a taxi to the airport."

"Only if we can spend the rest of the day reading on the beach," Monica sat back on her batik sarong and shielded the sun with her open book as she began to read. I moved over a few feet into the cool shade of a coconut palm and began to doze off.

As I gazed out of the corner of my eye I saw some eyes staring back at me through the undergrowth. Feeling quite startled I sat up and walked closer to investigate. The eyes grew slightly, closed, and a small boy quickly darted back through the jungle. I jumped into the shrubbery in pursuit, convinced this must be the same peeping eyes from the shower. I dodged roots and thorns as best as I could, but my soft Gringo feet were no match for the jungle trail—the boy kept just ahead of me. I wasn't about to give up, though. I ducked under a low branch and saw the boy make it to a clearing in the distance. I limped around the small meadow and entered the jungle again where the boy had gone. As I crawled through some thick ferns I saw him look back in my direction and recognized the face—it was Martin's son. His dark eyes scanned the clearing and I dropped lower into the green ferns. After a few seconds of watching the boy walked slowly, apparently believing he had lost his pursuer in the chase. I continued to follow at a distance, until the boy stepped into a well-concealed shack in the most remote and darkest part of the jungle on the island.

The shack had a thatched roof and stick walls, with only one small visible door that even the boy had to stoop to get through. Surrounding the hut were strange objects hanging in the trees. These hanging figures were wooden, made mostly of sticks, but they also had faces carved into soft coral with dark coconut husk hair and detailed features. The eyes were small black snail shells gouged into the ghostly coral faces. There were also strange fish teeth that were filed and poked into the coral around the mouth area. As I looked closer at the terrible looking little nasty monsters I lost my breath. What I had thought were sticks weren't sticks at all, but small, fragile bones. Maybe bird bones or fish bones. Maybe something larger like the bones from a hand, I couldn't quite tell. Even stranger were the open howling mouths of each little figure, which dripped a clot of drying blood. The blood looked like it had been layered on, day after day, for some time. And the coconut hair seemed also to be died dark with the blood of some poor creature.

My stomach churned inside as I looked at these devilish figurines, which seemed to completely surround the house. I didn't even notice that Martin had left the little shack and was walking toward me. A jungle bird screamed and brought me back to my senses just in time. I spun around and Martin grabbed me by my shoulders, but I slipped out of his grasp and took a step back. At this moment Martin recognized me and mumbled something.

"What are you doing here? You shouldn't be here." His eyes bugging wildly.

"I followed your son. He was spying on us. What is this place? And these things?" My mind was jumbled and I threw out these phrases, overlapped and fast.

"What?" Martin looked confused.

"I'm really freaked out. What is this?" I motioned to the dangling voodoo dolls or whatever they were.

"You won't understand. This is for the evil spirits. These things keep the spirits here and protect the island from any wandering demons. This house is the demon house. They stay here."

"What? What about the blood? The bones? Your son?" I questioned looking at the ground.

"I knew you wouldn't understand. My son has teeth filed to ward off the evil spirits. Western cultures don't understand this. The blood is necessary to keep the evil in."

"Well what kind of blood is it?" I looked closely at the dangling doll.

"You don't need to know. I told you you wouldn't understand." I saw a glimmer of something moving fast from the corner of my eye, but it is too late. Martin hit me hard with something on the side of my ear and I jerked my hand up to block the blow.

"Wake up, Al! You were twitching in your sleep. Come out and swim with me. It's too hot." Monica was pulling on my hand, to lead me to the water.

"Whoa." I shook my head, stunned by the reality of the dream, and grateful that it was only in my head. "I just had the weirdest dream. You will never believe what happened."

"Come and tell me about it in the water. This sun is hot." She led me out into the waves. As the sleep washed off I realized it was time to leave that place.

It is strange, but no matter how far in advance some people know about some important date or departure time, they still wait until the last minute to get ready. It's a little different than procrastination, really. That would be putting off the responsibility day after day. I suppose it is more of a subconscious love of panic and excitement right before a departure. I seem to do this sort of thing on a consistent basis for some reason. Running for taxis or busses. Sprinting through airports. That sort of thing.

Monica and I simply wanted to enjoy the beach as much as possible before the boat ride, taxi, 20 hour plane ride, and the long and depressing winter ahead of us in the States. We wanted to milk every last bit of the tropics, without the crumbling thoughts of reality and our inevitable return to it.

As usual, this left us sprinting toward the boat jetty, ten minutes before it was going to leave. No matter how I tried not to do this, these rushed departures always seemed to happen—like a receding hairline or something else in my genes.

My compulsive lateness seemed to be rubbing off, as well. My contagious tardiness must have had the death grip of the plague, because it even spread to the masters of punctuality—ze Germans were running down the trail beside us.

The four of us made quite a ruckus, sprinting toward the pier, our backpacks bouncing along behind us.

"It is a good thing Martin kept reminding us to keep our tickets in our pockets, I said between breaths, sweat burning in my eyes.

"Yeah," said Klaus. "Who's idea was it to 'carpe diem' on the beach until the boat came, anyway. 'To enjoy where we are and not worry about zhe journey.' How come we listened to you?"

"You had a watch. You could've gone early. You would have been sweating away by the pier next to the garbage pile," I huffed. We all were still in our swimming suits, having left our packs by the restaurant to milk the final beach hours.

"We are going to make it. Look, the boat hasn't left yet," Monica yelled from the front of the running line.

"I hope they don't care if our tickets got a little wet."

"I want to change clothes for the boat ride," Sabrina said. "I can't wear my wet swimming suit for the ride."

"I'll run to the boat and tell the boatman to wait! You can change by that shack on the beach," Klaus replied as he continued running down the pier to the boat.

We stopped and opened our packs to change, Monica wrapping a sarong around herself and pulling on some shorts and a tank top. I threw on some dry shorts and toweled off the sweat for the moment.

Sabrina squealed from the other side of the shack, then she continued yelling in German at Klaus who was now aboard the ship. As I jogged over to her she was tossing crumpled newspaper and white coral chunks out of her backpack.

"I've been robbed," she shouted. Sure enough, her bag was full of coral and news--weighted perfectly so she wouldn't even notice. "It was that man! He left my passport and credit cards, my shorts and shirt. He took everything else."

"Hey! Come now!" Klaus was screaming and waving like a mad man from the distant ship. "They are leaving now! They won't wait anymore!"

"We can't go back," I said. "Our plane leaves tomorrow. Do what you want."

Sabrina knew she had no choice. If she went back to confront Martin they would miss their plane ride home. She paused, whimpered, and tossed her empty backpack on her shoulders.

We all streaked for the boat, down the long wooden pier, the clear water sparkling all around us.

We jumped on the boat just as the captain untied the moorings, and we motored slowly out into the deep blue. I wiped the sweat out of my eyes, trying to catch my breath, and searched through my bag. Everything was still there, exactly like I left it.

"My stuff is all here," whispered Monica. "Money, passport, souvenirs. It's all here."

"Mine too." I looked at Monica who was trying her hardest to conceal her grin.

"Hey, my stuff!" Klaus was now yelling from the front of the creaking wooden boat as we hit the first wave. He began tossing coral and newspaper out of his pack, curing in German and English.

"No worries," I thought. "Card trick number 109. Steal the German's money, clothes, and even their high top trekking boots to sell in town. No worries, man."

FALLING FOR MILA

My foot lost its grip on the oily wooden rail of the dinghy, and my beautifully planned jump transformed itself into a stupid-looking, uncoordinated fall. The smell of old fish parts and motor exhaust filled my sinuses as I descended awkwardly toward the clear warm water. I was fifteen. I was feisty. I was macho. And I was about to be in big trouble. Again.

The tropical sun screamed down from high above, my stomach clenched, and my squinting eyes focused on the black objects directly beneath me. Genus echonisius: the black sea urchin, cactus of the sea. As I recognized the cool burst of an adrenaline triggered sweat, Mr. Sheldon sang out, "What in the hell is that kid..."and then his voice fizzled into the black and unknown bubble language of the South China Sea. My brilliant plan was as unsuccessful as any Bond villain's. And Mila had watched every aching minute of it.

Only Mila Zain could have produced the hormonal stuff that makes fairly normal teenage boys jump from tall boats into water housing twelve-inch poisonous needled creatures. Only Mila Zain. Mila, with melt in your mouth chocolate eyes. Eyes like baby deer. Mila, with nostrils that flared ever so slightly when she breathed her lovely breaths and melted honey lips that lured in lost butterflies with their grace and grandeur. Mila. Ah, just the sound of her name was worth the pain of an Everest of urchins. Her perfect, soft coffee skin and luxurious long hair teased my dreams, and her slight accent was a whispery jazz melody in a tropical breeze. Half-

Malaysian, half-Australian, she was a succulent, ripe mangosteen with the smooth red curves of the sandstone of Ayers rock.

It wasn't infatuation. That was much too long a word to describe the shortness of breath that I felt. I was in love. Or lust. Or something that hit me like a raging pink rhinoceros and left me wondering which way was reft and light and dup and woooowwwn. Mila. Oh.

We were on the boat as part of a weeklong field trip to the exotic Pulau Babi Besar, off of the east coast of Malaysia. We were students at the International School of Kuala Lumpur and our group was spending the day island hopping with our snorkeling gear. For our expedition the school chartered a local fishing boat to motor from tiny island to island to examine spectacular reefs, explore dense jungles, and lounge on sparkling white beaches. It was on this particular fateful trip that I elected to impress Mila with my pre-pubescent Evil Kenievel manliness.

Mr. Sheldon was our white haired leader who nagged us constantly with his breath of rotten avocados. He used the same warnings in the out of doors as he did in the chemistry classroom, shouting out phrases like, "No funny business, now. You're spinning your wheels, people." As if we were people. We were in the prime of our lives, super-human and indestructible.

Mr. Sheldon, in his tight-pants-helium-whine voice, had frequently warned us of being extra cautious around sea creatures. He cautioned of moray eels, tiger fish, sharks, and urchins. To me, the fact that the water contained harmful objects only added to the *braviosity* of my stunt; each dangerous creature added extra points to the difficulty of my dive. I crept up to the top of the fishing boat, planning out my deep-water landing. I took into account the wind, boat speed, and trajectory. My plan was working out perfectly. Mila would be watching when I unleashed my deep Tarzan yell and dove. Then, the big slip.

The fall must have looked pretty exciting from below, like watching somebody crash hard on the ski slopes while watching from the safety of the chair lift or watching a soccer game and seeing two players collide without seeing each other from the security of the stands. It is always half funny to watch things like that from a different perspective and then go about eating a bit of popcorn or something. It is never the same when you are the one being snickered at, the reason the old ladies have to cover up their eyes, so they don't see what happens next.

When I fell for Mila I pushed the emergency eject button on my chances of ever making it into the cool crowd. It would permanently blast me up and float me back down with a parachute into the category of loser and half-wit where I was already quite accustomed to dwelling. The fall cost me years of self-consciousness and insecurities that were only later dissipated by subsequent stunts and brave acts. Stunts like asking a girl a question and then actually listening. Brave acts like just being myself and not jumping off any moving objects.

So anyway, Mr. Sheldon pulled my shaking body back into the greasy boat with the help of a few other students. I was biting my lip to keep the blood-melting scream that was building up inside of me. I took a deep breath. Opened my eyes. I looked down in horror at the scene, fully aware of what I would see, like a person walking backward in a slasher-horror movie while the piano plays in a minor key. Six or seven shish kabob sized needles were poking an inch into my foot. I was nauseated, but the strange thing was, as I remember, the spines didn't hurt quite as much as I had expected. In fact, the pain wasn't half the torture Mr. Sheldon had warned us about.

Then the poison began to creep out.

My foot was an inferno and lava flowed through my veins, increasing steadily and multiplying like rush hour traffic on an LA freeway. The suntanned Malaysian boat captain offered to relieve his bladder onto my foot, which was apparently a folk remedy for urchin poison. I opted for letting nature take its dreary course. The fisherman settled for pounding the area with the wooden end of a hammer until the spines were in tiny fragments. I grimaced. I gritted. I looked toward Mila for support, for some sort of consolation for a brave effort. And she was as spectacular as ever, illuminated like a Goddess in the sunlight. Tears, which weren't Mila's, began to overflow as she glanced at me, then my foot, then back at me.

"Wow. What were you thinking? How stupid," her words stabbed

deep. To the hilt. Then twisted around in some verbal hara-kiri madness.
I slouched back praying that the misty hand of unconsciousness would grab
me, or at least hit me on the head with a big stick like the Malaysian
fishermen did with his morning catch.

The rest of the trip was ruined. What a fool I had been. I sat in a
tropical paradise, surrounded by coconuts and papayas ready to be plucked,
crystal lagoons boasting millions of wildly colored fish and miles of
exploitable jungle trails--and I played Uno with Mr. Sheldon. I sat and
rubbed meat tenderizer into my foot, lying there in misery, as Mila flirted
with Bruce Buehler. Bruce was the most boring guy in the entire class.

THE BIG MONEY WHEEL

On Wednesday I left home eating a piece of wheat toast with the crust cut off. It wasn't that I disliked the crust. Actually, I am quite fond of the brown stuff, but when I was young my mother always cut off the crust as if it were somehow like a banana peel or plastic wrapper that needed to be removed. I still do it.

When I left I didn't know where I was going. I had nowhere to go to. Leaving that place was just another item on a long list of things to do before I died, and who knows when they will eat their last piece of wheat toast? It could be on a Thursday.

I picked up my bag and walked to Carey's for a final cup of coffee and an hour to straighten out my ideas about the future. Or at least the rest of the day. The morning was icy, the mud ruts near the road frozen and crunchy to walk on. The air was dry and reddened with the smell of the last falling maple leaves and I felt the inside of my nostrils burn in the cold.

As I walked I noticed that every car that passed me was a pick-up. Some were new, but most rusted and grumbling. At one point in my life I had thought of so many trucks as a strange thing, but I had stayed long enough that I rarely noticed anymore. This thought reconfirmed my inner rumblings that reminded me I had lived in Pleasant Meadow for too long. I suppose it was a good time to move on.

In Carey's I pulled up at a circular stool at the bar, gave a spin as if it was a roulette wheel predicting my future, and slowed it down with my finger like the big money wheel on some television program. My grand prize was red vinyl and I plopped myself down.

What'll it be, Mr.? Said the short lady behind the counter. She had pins in her yellow hair to keep it out of her face. Her eyes were sad but painted to look happy, and she had tributaries of wrinkles leading to the river of the eye. At one point in her life her eyes must have smiled much more than the present.

Well, Donna, how about a coffee. I quietly reminded myself to never have a job that required a name badge. There should be a requirement that two people should have to talk before they know each other's names.

That it? Nothing else? She whispered loudly.

No thank you.

Cold out, huh?

Yeah. It freezes my nostrils.

Me too. Just wait 'til January. I'll be in Vegas by then. You couldn't pay me to stay here.

Maybe I'll come join you, I said and grinned. She looked at her ordering notebook, blushed, and I realized she thought she had been too friendly or talked with me a little bit too long.

Milk with that? She asked looking at her order book and not at me.

No, thank you. Donna moved down the counter and out to the tables that were mostly empty. She danced a wet rag on tables that needed no cleaning. The sun shone in at an angle and spotlighted the saltshaker on the table closest to the window. It could possibly have been the prettiest saltshaker I'd ever seen. My stare on the light blurred and focused and blurred again. I was hypnotized. I wanted to stare at the sparkling saltshaker all day long.

Here you go, Donna said loudly. She slid the coffee cup over to me and winked hard enough to make the tributaries deepen for a split second. She sniffed softy and walked back to the kitchen.

I walked south out of town and poked out my thumb. The first semi-trailer that passed by slowed down and eventually stopped. I was lucky. It was still cold.

Where you headed?

South toward Richland.

I can take you to Wellsburg then I'm turning east.

Great.

I swung up into the steamy cab and slammed the heavy door behind me.

I needed a lift a few times myself in my days, the trucker said. What's your name?

Dylan, I replied.

I'm Bob. He paused. I liked learning a name by hearing it better than reading it. It seemed more real. You like music?

Yeah, I do, I said.

Well seeing how it's my rig I should get to choose the music. But since I'm a gracious fellow I'll give you a choice. You want country or western? I blinked and Bob chuckled a low rumble from beneath his wild black beard.

He was a weird-looking guy. It seemed the bottom half of his body didn't match the top. He had dark glasses, an explosion of hair all over his face and neck, and a black mesh baseball cap pulled down low. He had an enormous chest and round belly that nestled up against the steering wheel like a soft watermelon. His black shirt was short sleeved and he wore a black leather vest, even in the cold weather, because he kept the temperature at a pleasant Floridian climate inside the silver Kenworth diesel. His forearms were hairy and thick. The tattoos under the hair were unidentifiable, partly because of the dark undergrowth and partly because they were old and smeared, like someone rubbed them with a wet thumb. Bob's bottom half was strangely narrow in size. His calves were Popsicle sticks, his thighs disappeared into his cushioned seat, and his backside appeared to be lacking completely. I wanted to ask if perhaps he lost his buttocks in a bizarre hunting accident or a land mine in Viet Nam, but his upper half was too much like a Hells Angel for me to be that courageous. Yet, the more I thought it through, the more I realized that if I sat around all day listening to music and eating chicken fried steak and Denver omelets my body might look the same way.

We rumbled down the highway to the harmonious Oak Ridge Boys for the entire morning. The heater made me want to sleep and have nice dreams of Buh Buh Buh Bobbie Sue, and I must have actually dozed for a while, because I woke up with a spot of drool on the side of my mouth and my head up against the big, padded door.

Do you know what the last thing that went through that bug's head was? Bob bellowed. He was pointing at a faded, yellow splattering on the windshield and he looked over at me while his Blue Blocker shades reflected a miniature version of my own face back at me.

I sat up straight, wiped my mouth a bit, and blinked slowly.

His ass. He chuckled slowly and loudly enough to cover up the music and the roaring engine. I smiled and nodded, and he continued to laugh. I feel more comfortable around people who laugh at their own jokes with such vigor. I certainly couldn't do that.

Well, it's time for the king, groaned Bob as he ejected the tape from the player.

Elvis? I asked.

Not on your life. The man was a disgrace. Too many drugs and women screaming for him. His pants were too tight and his music was too loud. I'm talking about Kenny.

Kenny? My sleepy brain grasped for meaning.

Rodgers. Now that man has class. No hip gyrations from him.

He also has a chain of chicken restaurants, I added.

Of course he does, countered my trucker companion. With a face like that who wouldn't stop for a few wings and a dinner? I stop at every Kenny Roasters restaurant I see to pay homage to the gambler. I'm telling you, every lesson a man needs to learn in life he could learn by listening to Kenny Rodgers. You gotta know when to hold em, know when to walk away, know when to run, islands in the stream is what we are.... the list goes on and on. It is some pretty deep talk he's talkin. I ain't read the Bible too much, but I tell you that I follow the word of Kenny Rodgers and I've been working out life's mysteries and problems just fine.

I nodded my head and kept my mouth shut.

Have you seen Six Pack? Asked Bob.

What?

Six Pack?

I've seen a lot of six packs, Bob.

No, I mean the movie.

Can't say that I have. Is it new? I haven't seen many new movies.

No, Bob grumbled impatiently. It is a classic. It is about this car racer who is great with kids. In fact, these kids are a real handful, but he is still great with 'em. You know why he is great with kids?

Why, Bob? I had a feeling I knew the answer but I wanted to give him the benefit of the doubt.

Because the car racer is a man with a silver beard and all of the answers. That is why. It is Kenny Rodgers. He's an actor and a singer too. Can you believe it? Who'd a thunk it? I'm telling you, the man is amazing. Do you know why I painted my truck silver? It weren't no coincidence. He should open a church up. The church of Kenny. I'd go. Wouldn't you? He glared at me with his eyebrows in a V, disappearing into his dark glasses.

Uh, sure, I coughed as I scratched my forehead; I'd give it a try.

Bob pushed in a new tape and we basked in the sun's and Kenny's warm glow, by means of a song about Lady. The frozen mile markers slipped by.

Where did a name like Dylan come from anyway? Bob asked me a few minutes later. I lied and said that I didn't know.

Bob dropped me off in Wellsburg with a gush of airbrakes and a hairy handshake.

Take this Kenny Rodgers tape and pass it along to someone who needs direction, Bob said loudly. It may not change the world overnight, but it sure has answered some questions for me.

Thanks, Bob, I replied and slipped the tape into my bag. I slammed the big door and as I walked away I heard him yell out of the passenger window.

Good luck on your trip, and watch out for daytime friends and nighttime lovers.

I couldn't have found a ride in Wellsburg if my life depended on it. People looked at me as if I were a monster. Or a child molester. I figure it must have been about three o'clock because the kids were out of school and walking home dragging their little backpacks full of books. It reminded me of my younger days, when I walked home every day.

There were yellow lights flashing and a sign that said school zone speed limit 20 mph. The cars were crawling past the crosswalks and I decided not to try to hitchhike near the town. My luck would be better outside of town near the freeway. I wanted no trouble with the locals.

As I walked past the old man crossing guard he grabbed my arm.

Here, can you help me out a second? My name's Ed, Ed Highbrazo. I gotta help my sister Erma get down to the hospital and I need someone to cover the crosswalk for a few minutes.

Me? I questioned, surprised that he would ask a complete stranger to relieve him of his duties.

Yes, you, said the old man. He handed me his reflective orange jacket and passed over the hand help stop sign as if it were the Holy Grail. Use it wisely, he said, and limped away toward the blue house on the corner.

I was in shock with the idea of my new responsibility and safety implements in this strange little town, but then shaken to my senses by a toothless little kid with a green shirt and a cowlick splitting his bangs down the middle.

Ekthuwz me mithter. I need to croth. Pleath.

He tugged on my pant leg with the rhythm of a Texas oil-well pump. This kid was alone. There were groups of students walking together, but he was a loner. His feet looked strange and when I looked closer I noticed that he was wearing his shoes on the wrong feet.

Your wearing your shoes on the wrong feet, I told him.

That ith exthactly what my mom saiths, the kid replied. I have tried putting them on the other way, but it feelths much better thith way. Have you tried wearing them like thith?

I had to be honest. No, I said, I haven't.

Try it.

O.K., I answered, I will sometime.

Try it now. It'th much more comfortabler. He let go of my leg, reached down, and began untying my left shoe.

Wait, I grunted, I'm working.

It doethen't take that long. I saw that nobody needed to cross at the moment so I gave in to the toothless munchkin and swapped my shoes.

Thsee? Isthen't that much better? He looked up at me and smiled hugely.

Oooh, yeah, I said and played along with comments of pleasurable comfort. I like this much better, I groaned, and danced a small jig. How did you discover this method of shoe wearing?

I juthed dithcovered it. Nithe ithen't it?

Yehes, I replied and walked to the center of the road, lifting my newly assigned, hand held, octagonal responsibly in the air. It's OK to cross now, son.

Thankth, Mithter, he replied and skipped across the street to the safety of the sidewalk.

When he arrived he jumped up into the arms of a well-dressed, middle-aged woman with a terrible scowl on her face. I smiled and waved with my hand that wasn't holding the stop sign, but received only a nastier scowl from the woman.

You should be ashamed of yourself, buddy! Making fun of my kid! She looked down at my shoes and literally spit on the sidewalk. Where is Mr. Highbrazo anyway? Who the hell are you? Some pedophile kidnapper? What have you done with Mr. Highbrazo, the cross guard?

I'm just helping him, I stammered. This woman was a volcano who had been sleeping for thousands of years and I suddenly realized that I was the village of innocent tropical islanders who were eating mangos as the first spouts of lava and the pyroclastic flow began racing down the hill.

I'm not from here. Just passing through, I squeaked.

A stranger? Helping our kids? Where is Mr. Highbrazo? Don't even try to move. I'm calling the cops. She switched bladed her cell phone open and dialed three numbers.

Wait! I screamed.

You wait! She screamed, pointing a crooked finger at my head, making the scene appear like some kind of an imaginary gun crossing guard stick-up. Don't move!

But I had to move--I was standing in the middle of the road. Even though I had the stop sign up I had a long line of cars that were waiting impatiently, beginning to honk, and looking concerned. She was talking with the police.

In a fit of desperation I dropped the sign and ran back to the corner by the school. I looked left and right and then ran to the only place I recognized--the crossing guard's blue house.

I figured that nobody would be home. The crossing guard was most likely in the hospital by now with his sick sister, and I couldn't waste valuable time knocking on doors that wouldn't be opened. So, I took the liberty to walk in like I owned the place.

The air inside was stale and smelled of the elderly. The room was pink. In fact, everything was pink: the carpet, the floral wallpaper, the silky curtains, and the couch--all varying colors of pink. To my surprise, on a lazy boy recliner in the corner, sat Mr. Highbrazo, his feet up and a can of root beer condensing beads of sweat on the arm rest.

What are you doing here? We echoed off of the pink wallpaper in unison. Highbrazo coughed. Why aren't you helping the kids across the street? I gave you a job to do.

I left, I replied. I just met you, Mr. It is not my job. By the way, what are you doing here and where is your sister? Emma, right?

Erma. She is not here. She is dead. Where is my stop sign?

What are you talking about? I left your stop sign in the road. I was running for my life. What are you doing?

I'm watching the Price is Right.

Well I can see that. But why? You should be helping kids across the street. It is your job. Now I'm in trouble. There is a lady after me--and probably the cops by now. I'm in big trouble.

I'll say you are--why aren't you doing your job!

My job? Are you kidding? It's your job! I just met you. And now I'm in trouble, and you are watching Bob freaking Barker. I thought you had to help Edna.

Look, he said, and took a swig of cool root beer; I've got to explain something.

Yes, you do. Many somethings, I replied.

See, my sister isn't really sick. In fact, she died seven years ago. But I love this TV program and it just so happens that it is on at the same time as when the kids get out of school. I only get to watch the first ten minutes every weekday. Ten minutes! Do you know how painful that is? I never get to see the final round where they win the big money. I just hear the "come on down" part and then I'm off with my stop sign and orange vest.

You have got to be kidding me. Your sister is dead? The Price is Right? I must be dreaming. I pinched myself and it hurt. I'm in trouble, Mr. The police might be after me.

What do you mean, police? What did you do? Are you a criminal or something?

No! I was just helping you. I am in trouble because I was doing *your* job.

Whoa, now. Wait a minute. There is nothing illegal about my job. I just help kids across the road.

Please, you have got to help me. I didn't do anything wrong. I was just trying to help you. I can explain in the car. I promise. Do you have a car?

There was a long pause in which I could hear the words "a new car" on the television. The man finally lowered the leg rest on the lazy boy, finished off his root beer, and turned to me.

Yeah, and I suppose I owe you, but you have to drive. I can't see well enough. Depth perception problem, you know. The car is out back here.

So I drove the rusty royal blue Chevy Nova south with Mr. Highbrazo. He said if we were pulled over he would announce that he wasn't a hostage, but an old friend of mine. He announced that we could head to his sister Joy's house and be there in just under an hour. Joy would then drive him back home and he would explain to the police just what had happened. I nodded in agreement, and pressed on the accelerator.

.

ALEX PETERSON

THE PURE BLISS OF A WEED FREE YARD

The yard is more than orderly; it is standing at attention. The tulips march in file and the shrubbery have crew cuts. The grass never exceeds two and one-quarter inches, and the edges are chopped weekly with a gas powered edging tool. Elm trees never slouch, roses bloom in schedule, barely daring to have thorns, and earthworms cower at the thought of intruding into the local ground space.

These grounds are sprinkled each morning at 5:30 sharp with mineral rich water and the help of an electronic timer system, and then sprinkled again at 8:30 PM when the sun is down and with it the threat of moisture loss due to evaporation. Ship-shape, tidy, and uncluttered--the flowerbed is arranged in layers, like a healthy lasagna on its side. First, a low wire fence with an intricate lace design keeps unsightly grass intrusions from the unsoiled soil. Next, a series of medium sized river rocks are placed strategically on the outer perimeter of the flower bed, a fortress of stone steadfastly protecting the tulips of alternating colors: wine, ivory, wine, ivory, wine, and so on. The entire front yard is an exquisite masterpiece, hardly a thing to be trifled with, and the burning envy of the entire neighborhood. Except for the Srugsays.

It is true that Srugsay is a peculiar name--definitely not one measured by the foot in phonebooks like, Green, Brown, Smith, or Baker. Yet, Srugsay was their name. They refuse to normalize it.

Though the exact genealogy was a bit vague, the Srugsay name surely stemmed from predominantly, or even pure, Bohemian stock. That is, if there exists a pure Bohemian. And as for where Bohemia is or was--that is irrelevant because this story takes place in America, and half of US citizens don't even know what countries share his or her own border. More specifically, the setting here is in the suburbs of America. It could be anywhere really: West, East, or Middle, because suburban environments tend to be similar. A strip mall is a strip mall and isn't usually known for its eclectic or unique features, if you know what I mean. One can walk into a Seven-Eleven or a Starbucks anywhere in the USA and know exactly where to find the Slurpees or the half and half.

The Srugsays are a wholesome clan, lovers of nature and protectors of green things and free living. The rest of the block must think it odd that such an open-minded, earthy type of family (often referred to as *tree-huggers, hippies*, and more often than not *stinking Birkenstock wearing dirt bags* by these very neighbors) would pick the clean-cut suburban sprawl in which to reside. Most of their types would prefer a more classical or retro environment in which to dwell peacefully, letting their ponytails and/or armpit and leg hair grow and not be confined by the cold suburban nether regions of America.

But the Srugsays are different. They are not content with merely settling between other liberal minded people--they want to be voyagers on the ideological frontier. The Srugsays want to live life on the edge. They wish to be a thorn in the side of the establishment, valiant flag bearers of organics, and sharers of any knowledge which enlightens minds in the struggle against women haters, alternative lifestyle bashers, Superbowl watchers, and Mega-low-marts everywhere.

The Srugsays just so happen to live next door to the aforementioned neighbors with the immaculate yard. And, as you may now sense, there is a trickle of tension arising in the space between these two neighbors. The horticultural handiwork (wine, ivory, wine, ivory) is perfected by the Wrights, Tamera and Otis; but, mainly Otis. Tamera, or Tammy, is usually busy inside. They are a law abiding and middle-aged couple. They enjoy chips, chicken pot pie, baby carrots, and celery sticks with a light and creamy dip. Their one son, Mac, is the quiet type of teenager who mostly stays in his room. Otis especially likes to listen to AM radio as he prunes and trims. It sooths him. Tammy is a big fan of Oprah. Oh, yes, and Otis is the manager of the Mega-low-mart down the street past the old mall.

As the story begins Mrs. Wright is emptying the contents of her off-white refrigerator into the big black garbage can outside of the house. Otis is meticulously trimming the curbside lawn edge with a pair of pruning shears that resemble a massive pair of scissors.

"Otis," Mrs. Wright calls adjusting the white curlers above her ear, "there is something wrong with the fridge. I found several oranges with a spots of green mold. How putrid. I am tossing everything. You know how fungus spreads. The entire fridge is basically a den of fornicating bacteria now."

"What honey? I can't understand you with my headphones on," Mr. Wright replies pulling at the reverberating sound of Rush Limbaugh as it oozes into the air around his large ears. His wife repeats her discovery and Mr. Wright reacts with a blend of perplexity and anger. "What about the hot dogs? I just bought them yesterday!" Wright roars from his kneeling position, inhaling deeply on the cigarette, which dangles precariously from his thin lower lip.

"Are they opened?"

"Yeah, but I only ate a few."

"Sorry. They are gone." She lobs the franks gently into the big black can with an underhand backspin toss.

"Damn oranges," Wright grunts, stabbing his trimmers into the lawn like a weird landscape architecture version of a Hitchcock shower scene. "They probably brought them in from California or Mexico..." Stab. Stab. "...just ready to mold."

Just then the back door of the Srugsays' house opens and out runs Sierra, the youngest of the family, at full speed. Behind her is a black Labrador, Garcia, excited, and frothing out a short string of slobber that yo-yos down his jowls.

"Eaachkhooey," screams the wild child, barefooted, blazing through the long grass self-propelled and half hovering, the wind in her hair. In her hand she holds a pink mutilated Frisbee, glistening with something wet and clear, high above her wild curly mane. Garcia bounces behind her, like an insane, small, black deer. He obviously realizes he can't jump high enough to snatch his tooth marked toy, but he is poised for the slightest chance to nab his chewy disc if the girl by chance lets it down a bit too low.

The girl runs a short lap around the maple tree in the back yard and streaks back toward the house in a blur. Otis Wright looks up from his grass grooming just in time to see the girl trip on an exposed root, sail through the air, tumble, and land flat on her face in the grass. The ebony tornado now sees his opportunity and is instantly on her, wrestling the Frisbee from the girl's grasp. For a moment the scene is all a jumble of bare feet, fur, grass, and dog slobber. Then Garcia rises from the carnage-- the victor.

Mrs. Wright looks over at the scene and gasps, her hands covering her freshly glossed lips. She takes a step toward the fallen girl, but Sierra is up on her feet again, like a stunned wild animal. She is now giving chase to the black dog, which is running madly in front of her carrying the ravaged Frisbee in his mouth.

"EEhhyooyaow!" the child shrieks, disappearing beyond the house.

"That feral child needs an upbringing," Mrs. Wright says.

"That kid needs medication," her husband mumbles. "And that dog is probably rabid or full of ring worm or something. It is deranged."

"Just like the owners," comments Mrs. Wright. "Just like the owners. You would think the girl was raised by..."

"Sierra!" Mrs. Srugsay enters the story, opening the back door and calling for her child. Come in and eat! Your banana buckwheat pancakes are getting cold." As Janis Srugsay scans the backyard for her daughter she sees the Wrights staring at her across the driveway.

"Good mmmorning," she says. "Have you seen my energetic daughter this morning?"

"Yes," Mrs. Wright pauses. "She was being attacked by that big black dog of yours just a minute or two ago in your back yard."

"Oh, thank you! I'll just keep looking." Janis nods, repeating her daughters name with her motherly calls. Janis Srugsay is a lanky woman, lean from years of yoga stretching and whole grains. She has pretty blue eyes like tropical water and long brown hair that she constantly pushes back behind her soft ears. Her nose is sprinkled with a constellation of freckles and her peaceful motions resemble the leaves of a strong tree blowing in a gentle breeze.

She walks back into the house, putting two smallish pancakes on a plate, and pours a spoonful of rich, creamy honey on top of them. She sits down at the table and sips fresh black coffee from a steaming ceramic mug. The light from the early morning spotlights her mug and hand through the kitchen window and Janis notices that her long fingers have the same curvature as her mother and also her daughter. They are not weak hands. She breathes in a calming breath and exhales through her nose, smiling slightly at the same time.

Through the window Janis can now see Sierra playing with Garcia in the beautiful yellow flowers in the front yard. They both look so happy, rolling in the dandelions, wrestling for the Frisbee.

Janis walks to the front door and calls out into the lovely springtime air, "Breakfast, Sierra!"

The girl looks up and smiles a huge mouthed snaggly toothed grin and nods at her mother. As Janis looks closer she notices that the dog has a brilliant yellow ring around his neck where Sierra has stuffed dandelion stems under the worn collar.

"Look, Mom, Garcia has a flowler necklace."

"That's marvelous honey. I like it. Now come in and we'll eat. And bring me one of those big yellow flowers will you?"

As the girl bounces through the doorway she is nearly out of breath.

"Mom," she wheezes, "Our yard is so full of flowlers. Everywhere. Here. Take a big one for you."

"These are called dandelions, dear. *Taraxacum offinale*. These flowers are self-fertilizing. They create themselves. Amazing, huh? And if you know how to do it right you can eat the stems and leaves or make them into dandelion wine. The name is taken from the French words meaning 'lion's teeth.' They energize and tone our body. They are high in vitamin A, iron, potassium, and much more." At this point there is a thin glaze that comes over Janis Srugsay's eyes as she concentrates on the regurgitation of past knowledge and she entirely forgets the mental capacity of her audience. "These flowers are a diuretic, a coffee substitute (heaven forbid), a liver cleanser, and even a cholagogue. A chologogue, of course, being a substance that aids in digestion by increasing the bile flow from the gall bladder." She shakes her head quickly, the glaze fades, and Janis stands looking down once again at her daughter. "Your daddy even likes to eat dandelions on his salad in the springtime, with a nice Roquefort dressing."

It is likely that now would be a good time to explain that Janis Srugsay is not only an avid botanist, but she is finishing up her dissertation material on homeopathy and ancient herbal remedies; thus her experience with the medicinal qualities of many herbs and botanical cures, and the reason for her knowledge of the word "cholagogue."

"Oh yeah," Sierra rambles, completely oblivious to her mother's scientific ramblings, "Mr. Wright says he wants to talk to Dad about something. He told me to tell you."

"OK, dear. Now eat your pancakes. Also this yogurt, apricots, and wheat germ. I'll tell your dad when he gets back from his fifteen mile run," Janis says as she scoops yogurt liberally next to her daughter's buckwheat pancakes.

****

Yvon Srugsay runs briskly, with a joyful hop in his step, like he is five years old again and trying out a pair of new sneakers to see how fast they are. His face is slender and tanned and handsome. His body is wiry and weathered. He is a triathalete.

He rounds the corner and sprints the home stretch--only half a mile left to go.

Upon arrival Yvon observes how his house stands out from the rest. He relishes the unique spirit of his home, realizing that these conformist suburbs are not exactly a nexus of individuality. His house is different. It's not only different--it is bright purple. The windows are festooned with stained glass and wind chimes from around the globe, and the front door was hand painted by Yvon himself. The front yard is a creation of Janis-- well, actually, a creation of Pacha Mama, Mother Nature herself; but, with a bit of care and extra watering by Janis.

"Let's let whatever grows grow and not trim and cut everything!" she proposed one summer. And so it was. The yard was a free growing, occasionally watered refuge for whatever wanted to live there.

"It is beautiful," Yvon says out loud.

As he reaches his home he notices how the dandelions have exploded in bloom all over the yard: gorgeous yellow complimenting the purple house--utterly divine. The peaceful moment doesn't last long.

"Srugsay," blurts out Mr. Wright from his porch as Yvon runs by. "How are you? Can I speak with you a minute. I've got a bit of a concern."

"No problemo, neighbor. What can I do?" Yvon Srugsay halts his trot and begins stretching his calf muscles.

"Do you need some 24D? Roundup?" Wright asks bluntly.

"Excuse me?"

"Poison. Weed poison. For your grass. I realize that this is a free country and you have the right to enjoy whatever type plants, well, almost any type of plants, in your own yard. But in any wind those yellow bastards are likely to spread out across the entire neighborhood and ruin all of our yards--yards we work hard on to keep nice."

"Hmmm." says Srugsay.

"And I'm just asking if you want to borrow some poison to tame those weeds. For control. The other neighbors might not be so nice.

You're liable to ruin the entire neighborhood if your plants start to spread--especially the ones in the front that everyone can see. Personally, I don't care what you grow in the back--that's your business. But, the front makes the whole neighborhood look shabby. And like I said--your stuff is likely to spread."

"Well thank you for your input neighbor. I'll consider your proposal. But might I ask why you consider this beautiful yellow flower the enemy? Dandelions? What is wrong with them?" Srugsay responds inquisitively.

Wrights eyebrows rise and he blinks quickly a few times in astonishment.

"Look, I don't know what kind of an upbringing you had, but the rest of us around here don't like those weeds. They spread like wild fire and the parachute seeds blow all over," Wright pauses, catching his breath. "I could even come and spray them for you, if you don't want to deal with the 24D. I'll even pay for it--on sale at Mega-low-Mart, you know."

"Hold on! Let me think about this. We are trying to let the yard grow naturally and I'm not sure how natural this 24D poison is. We want natural." Srugsay says politely, but defensively.

"You can say that again--no, you already did. Natural as a freakin' jungle. We'll be seeing monkeys in your trees soon." Wright is getting irritated. "I could cut and bale your lawn while I am at it."

"Don't get too hasty. Let me talk this all over with Janis and we will figure something out. I'm sure there is a logical solution." And with that Yvon Srugsay turns around and walks straight into Garcia, the big black dog, who is offering up the slobbery remains of a Frisbee to be chucked into the back yard.

"What is this, Garcia?" Srugsay bends down and observes the dog is covered in a ring of bright yellow flowers.

*****

Otis Wright slams the side door hard as he enters the house; so hard, in fact, that Mrs. Wright leans her head in from the TV room, interrupting her viewing of Oprah, to see what all of the commotion is about.

He quickly pulls a cigarette from the front pocket of his beige golf shirt and lights it with the strong yellow flame of a Zippo.

"I've had enough! I tell you, Tammy, that man won't be satisfied until my yard and the whole neighborhood is in ruins," Wright exclaims. "In fact it's not even him! He isn't even man enough to make the decisions for the family. He's in there 'conferencing' with the real boss of the family right now and she is telling him that the yard needs no controlling. She probably never had a yard, growing up in the circus or carnival or whatever drug addicted commune she came from."

"Now Otis..." comes a faint voice from the TV room. "Stop your ranting. I'm trying to watch this poor girl from Taiwan who was sold for a pocket watch and a bag of rice."

There is a pause and Otis hears her take a long sip of Diet Coke as it bubbles through the straw and finally lets out a rattling slurp at the bottom of the glass.

"No, Tammy. I'm not going to relax as my yard is overrun with those damn weeds. This yard is my joy. I worked my way out of the apartment complex so I could enjoy a yard of my own. I'm not a bad guy--I'm no square. I just like my yard my way. If those Srugsays want to ruin their own yard and make it look like the disgrace of the town—let them. I wish they would show some pride, but let them. But I need to take matters into my own hands." Otis Wright draws in deeply as the red glow of his Marlboro edge toward his fingertips. He hasn't always been an angry man, but he's made a decision to never be pushed around again. He has come a long way from his bullied youth in Cleveland.

"Whatever dear. Do what you want. Oprah is almost over," comes the mindless reply from the other room.

Wright looks out of the window. "She doesn't understand," he mumbles to himself. "Something has got to be done. Somebody has got to do something. Take action." He burns two more Marlboros, sitting patiently in quiet cogitation at the kitchen table. The smoke curls skyward, a gray sidewinder in the springtime sunlight and all is quiet except for Otis' deep breathing and the background clapping of the audience on the television.

The quite is interrupted by the telephone. Otis lets it ring three times, though it is within easy reach. He is relaxed again. Almost.

"Otis, can you get it?" squeals Tammy.

He glares into the other room with a look of a teenager asked to clean his room, squints his eyes, and repeats his wife words back at her silently.

Otis snatches the phone forcefully and slams it to his ear. "Wright here. Go ahead."

"Hey, neighbor!" The voice registers like a dentist's drill or a splinter stabbing into the flesh under Wright's fingernail. "I've talked it over with Janis and Sierra here and we've reached a decision."

There is a drawn out pause and Srugsay's voice sparks up again.

"Hello? Anyone there?"

"Yes," Wright replies with sarcastic abruptness. "What did *you all* decide?"

"Well, we want to be sensitive to your concerns about the dandelion issue."

"Good."

"But...quite honestly, we love our yard how it is--free. And we just don't see how it interferes at all with your yard, or anyone else's. What you may see as nasty weeds we happen to view as nice wild flowers, that just so happen...to be easy to grow. Do what you want to your property; but, we don't want any toxic substance sprayed on our lawn, being put into the air, soaking into the water supply, or poisoning our ecosystem. So our answer is regrettably, no."

Wright breathes out slowly. "Well, I'm sorry to hear that." He then lifts the phone receiver away from his ear, high in the air like an Olympic medal--and slams it hard onto the ringer.

"Otis? What are you doing in there? Did you drop something?" Mrs. Wright questions seriously, yet not motivated enough to actually get out of her lazy boy recliner and walk in to investigate the commotion.   "It's those damn, stinking hippie neighbors. They are going to ruin this neighborhood and all of the hard work I've put into this yard. Why? Because they think those dandelions are *pretty*. It's not enough to give a stinking cow or a chicken the right to live. Now those tree-hugging vegetarians are protecting the *weeds* in their yard. Why can't they just move to San Francisco or something and be with their own kind."

"Oh, Otis."

"NO! I won't let them destroy what I work for. It's my God given right! I'm going to sneak over their tonight and spray their yard with poison whether they like it or not."

There is a moment of silence in which Otis realizes that the TV is no longer on. His head turns slowly and his wife's voice squeals around the corner. "Otis Wright, you stop that talk immediately," Tammy's tone is fingernails on the chalkboard, amplifier feedback. Her inclemency is doubly reinforced when she appears from the depths of the TV room and walks straight up to the kitchen table, only inches from her husband's red face.

"Do you know how many lawyer friends the Srugsays have? Do you? Probably about half of their friends, dear. Half. Lawyers who take away people's houses because there is an "endangered" turtle found in their back yard. Lawyers that will take our money and car and house so fast it would make your thick head spin. You just put that idea right out of your head, Mr. And I mean it." Tammy stands tall, slowly swaying back and forth like a skyscraper in a strong wind.

Otis slumps back in his chair. He is still angry, but he knows his wife is right. If he sprayed their yard it wouldn't only kill the dandelions, it would kill all of the broad-leafed plants in the entire yard, and because the majority of the foliage was weed-like, there wouldn't be much left alive. He knows they would figure out the culprit easily, with Otis's warnings to

Srugsay and all.

"It just isn't right," Wright mumbles, flipping a new hard pack carton of Marlboro reds with his index finger. He opens up the package and quickly lights up. Halfway down the cigarette Otis Wright has a bursting flash of insight—genius, really, in his opinion.

"I'll cut them out," he thinks to himself, "I'll create a weed-pop-o'matic: a device that digs up the blasted yellow flowers by the roots and pops them out of the ground. This way I won't kill the entire yard and I can be rid of the weedy beasts forever. Srugsay will never know what happened. The dandelions will just disappear. It's perfect. I just need to create my pop-o'matic this evening and spend the night getting rid of the weeds."

"Otis?" his wife rummages through the cupboard for something to snack on. "Why not take the problem to City Council if it really bothers you this much? We have friends there. They will support you and the caring yard owners in town. By the way, have you seen the ranch flavor corn chips?"

"No, too much red tape, bureaucracy, and time for that honey. By the time they adjourned, the weeds would have spread all over. But don't worry. I'm going to try not to worry about it so much. There's nothing I can do. And no, I haven't seen the chips." When Otis looks away from his wife he is smiling. But his eyes glint with a hint of danger and a touch of madness. He breathes in another lengthy drag from his smoke and slowly taps his fingers consecutively on the tabletop.

"I'm glad to hear that you're not so worried about it. You can kill the weeds when they cross over into our yard."

"Yeah. OK, honey," Otis responds loudly. His eyes close slowly.

"Tomorrow night," he thinks to himself. "Tomorrow night I'll do it. They'll never know what happened."

"What happened, Janis, to the Subaru?" Yvon Srugsay calls from the front yard. It is the next day, in the afternoon, and he has just returned from his 23-mile bike ride from the office.

"I washed it, Dear," she replies. "Yes, it actually has been white all along underneath the dirt."

"Really," he jokes, and walks over and hugs his wife as she gets out of the car. "Where have you been?"

"I went over to Pat's botany lab at the university to check out some material for my thesis project. You'll never guess what I found. Come inside and I'll tell you what we're growing in our yard."

Sierra runs into the backyard as the couple enters the house and Janis begins immediately to ramble on in scientific jargon about something, while Yvon bends over, touching his palms to the floor in front of him.

"Now slow down here a minute, Einstein. Tell me in plain English what you are talking about." He kicks a foot up on the table and begins some hurdler stretches.

"OK," Janis takes a breath and calmly starts her story over again. "I noticed some abnormally large *Taraxacum offinale*, dandelions, in the front yard yesterday morning. As you are aware, Pat has her botany lab down at the university and she is always interested in strange or rare plants, so I dropped one of these huge flowers off for her to check out. Well, Sierra and I stopped by today for me to pick up some books at school and we ran into Pat. She asked us where on earth we collected the dandelion specimen and I told her.

"And..." Yvon chimes in, his arms locked behind his head like a fleshy pretzel.

"It so happens that she examined the sample and it is an extremely rare breed of dandelion. This type of plant has learned how to survive in a poisonous environment. They have adapted to constant spraying and genetically altered themselves to actually use the poisonous chemicals as food--nourishment. Yvon. Isn't it great?"

"You mean to tell me that these are some sort of mutant dandelions growing in our yard?"

"Exactly. I think that they have taken refuge here and grown stronger and stronger with all of the town and neighborhood spraying so much of that weed-free poison.

"Wow," Yvon stops his stretching and looks at his wife, his hands resting on his hips.

"And that's not all. These flowers, which happen to be five times the normal *Taraxacum offinale* size, carry with them 800-1000 seeds that will also be immune to poison, and actually eat 24D like Miracle Grow. Isn't it amazing? Survival of the fittest plant. Darwin would be proud--the old coot. Imagine--dandelions adapting to their environment like anti-biotic resistant germs."

"So even if someone killed all but one, this one flower could produce up to 1,000 new ones?" Yvon Srugsay questions.

"Yeah. And even more than that, when you pluck one of these the water supply is cut off and within six hours the dry seedpods are ready to detach and spread. Pat said she had to contain the seeds in a pod trap in her lab. Crazy, huh?"

"And these plants actually eat the poison?"

"Yep. Just like you enjoy carob soy dream and falafel on rye, these things dig Round-Up."

"This sounds like attack of the killer dandelions or something. We better not eat anymore young leaves on salad or the rest might get angry and attack." Srugsay comments with his hands up in the air, fingers curved, like a stuffed Grizzly on a hunter's cabin wall, ready to maul an innocent picnic.

"Isn't nature beautiful," Janis sighs as she carries her books into the bedroom.

Later that evening Otis Wright sits on his front porch in a folding lawn chair freshly purchased with his 25% employee discount from Mega-low-Mart. Along with the chair he purchased a pair of dark trousers, a black jacket, and a can of black bow hunter's face paint to better facilitate his blending into the night. He also purchased a small army light with a red lens and a new bottle of 24D broadleaf poison to spray his own lawn in case any seeds parachuted over accidentally in the breeze. He is ready. He is tranquil. He is a Japanese kamikaze pilot awaiting the sneak attack on the Pearl Harbor of plants. As he smokes calmly, Wright eyes the bedroom window of the Srugsays and strategically plans the frontal assault trajectory. As the Srugsays sleep peacefully, or count free-range sheep, they will never see him destroy the enemy. The dandelions will be plucked and carefully disposed of before dawn. He knows he will rest the next day with the pure bliss of a man with a weed free yard—the threat of encroachment having been completely annihilated.

As Otis rests his wrist on the lawn chair, rolling his cigarette slowly in between his finger and thumb, a flying object slightly resembling a Frisbee flies past his porch and skids to halt on his immaculate driveway, leaving a skipping trail of dog spit that sparkles in the red-orange sunset. Sierra Srugsay emerges from behind the maple in the back yard with a black shadow bouncing behind her. The dog takes the lead and pounces on the Frisbee, pushing it with his face, trying to get his nose under it and pawing to turn the mutilated thing over and get it into his mouth.

"Sorry, Mr." the young girl shrieks and grabs the dog in a strange wrestling hold. "Garcia. Come home!"

"It's OK. Don't worry," Otis says, making a mental note to wash the driveway off the next day. He notices the energy oozing from the young girl and he is strangely envious of her freedom. His father never would have let him run around outside after dinner on a school night.

Otis shakes his head and clears his thoughts. He realizes he needs to make an effort to be neighborly and not attract any more suspicion. "Tell your dad that we need to get together and have a barbecue sometime. There isn't any sense in us not being friendly neighbors. We could have hamburgers and hot dogs. I like hot dogs. Don't you?"

The girl stops in her barefooted tracks, looks at Wright with a cold glare and coughs. "We don't eat animals. Specially not hot dogs, Mr. Mama doesn't even let Garcia eat hot dogs."

"Oh, sorry."

The girl bursts into a smile, "but I like veggie burgers with ketchup."

"OK. Alrighty. We can make some veggie things, then."

Otis watches the girl skip away and he smoothly inhales the last draw of his Marlboro, shaking his head in shame at an American family that has never taken their kid to a baseball game to eat a hot dog. He continues shaking his head as he walks inside to take a short rest before the long night that was ahead of him with his newly invented weed pop-o-matic.

The next morning Otis Wright awakes with a jerk--a jerk on the toe, that is. He looks down to see his wife shaking his big toe, which is sticking out from under the blanket. On the floor, beside the bed, lie his new black clothes and his face is still slightly dark around his eyes where he failed to remove all of the bow hunter's make-up in the early morning hours. His mission is accomplished, a complete success. He has popped and bagged each of the dandelions in the neighbor's yard, covered his tracks, disposed of the ugly weeds in his own garbage can which would be taken out by the city garbage truck at 9:00 AM. He has done it all so masterfully, so stealthily, that he himself was smiling the entire time, just like the kleptomaniacs in Mega-low-Mart and exactly the same way he smiled after he bowled his first 250. It was all perfect, and the Srugsays had slept through the entire endeavor.

"Otis! Wake up. It's 7:30. There is something I have to tell you." Tammy is still tugging on his toe.

"What?" Wright mumbles groggily. "I'm tired."

"Well that Satan dog next door has knocked down the garbage can you put out by the road to be emptied and the entire mold infested contents of our fridge is scattered all over the front and back yard. I haven't put my contacts on yet, but it looks like that Mexican mold has turned the entire mess of food yellow!"

The panic spirals from Otis Wright's bobbing big toe through his body to his mouth, which makes him grasp for air. He runs outside to see if what he fears is true.

It is.

His lawn is littered, or rather covered, in garbage, debris, slobbery food leftovers, and dandelions, already in seed.

Wright quickly looks in the direction of his neighbor and sees that there is no sign of movement in the house yet. He knows they will be awake soon. He has got to move fast.

In an instant Otis Wright dashes to the garage and pulls out his padded handle rake and an extra thick black garbage bag. He moves like a stock car in the final lap, frenzied, but deadly accurate with his rake. Within nine turbo-charged minutes he has mopped up the entire mess, placing everything back in the garbage can, double bagged for safety.

He slumps back in his lawn chair and wipes the sweat from his forehead with a hairy forearm.

"That was close!" Otis groans, knowing that he has barely escaped a major disaster--being caught red, or rather yellow, handed--the bright evidence all over the front lawn.

"Too close," he mumbles to himself. "I better remember to spray another batch of 24D on the yard just to be sure all of those dandelion seeds die. At the same time I can sit here and guard the evidence from that rabid black mutt until the trash man comes at 9:00."

Peacefully, Otis lights up a celebration smoke. He has done it. It hasn't been easy, and with the scare this morning, he thought he was done for.

"And in the end the smart neighbors weren't as smart as they thought they were," he says to himself. Otis puffs up his chest, proud of his deed, and feeling confident in his new calling as some sort of vigilante anti-ecoterrorist. Now, all he has to do is enjoy his cigarette and guard the garbage can with its double-bagged contents and it will shortly be on its way to the county landfill--far, far away. He will soon go back to bed, free from worry, and enjoy the sleep and pure bliss of a man with a weed-free yard.

CROSSING THE BRIDGE

"Uh, dude, did you know that this is the longest bridge in the world?" Parsons mumbles loudly. Through the industrial haze, I can see the end of the rusty metal beams, and I know we will be off the bridge after two hundred more wing-tipped steps. The shining skyscrapers are distorted in the mirage of a blazing, mid-July sun. The air is heavy—not the pleasantly dry heat of the desert back home. The humidity hits hard, like a liquid linebacker, keeping the entire city on edge. It is Friday, but no TGIF is involved. We work on weekends, too. On days like today, we sometimes change shirts at lunch, due to a strange brown film that forms when large amounts of road dirt and pollution stick to our necks and our white, pressed shirts, like Shake-n-Bake sticks to slick chicken.

"What about the Golden Gate, Parsons?" I reply.

Parsons moans back, "No way, dude, this fetchin' bridge is longer."

"Give me a break, man."

"But this bridge starts in America . . . and ends in Africa." Parsons then proceeds to chortle heartily at his own joke, first slowly, then building to a modest idle, like an old trolling motor. The ability to laugh at and entertain himself for hours on end is one of the more admirable character traits of my large companion.

Elder Parsons (the redundancy of his name is not a subliminal clue to an extra pious personality) is from Idaho. He was bred on Jesus, roast beef, and potatoes. He can tell me the exact firepower and "military effectiveness" of nearly every post-World War II weapon invented. Parsons told me once that he was going to name his first child Remington and the next Winchester. I told him that was fine, but he had better stop having kids before he named one Glock. Wayne Parsons hates Cleveland. He hates everything about it—even the Indians, who have rallied from something like forty years of baseball misery to become the new American League contender in the World Series. Normally, disliking Cleveland would seem a perfectly acceptable and even common outlook, but we both know we will spend the next twenty months living as Mormon missionaries in what we term "the armpit of the nation." Parsons simply cannot come to terms with the fact that he is stuck here. He cannot wait until he gets home so he can join the police academy. "I want to be a cop to shoot people, mostly," he admitted to me one night while we talked after our routinely elegant Kraft dinner of macaroni and cheese, a.k.a. mac and yak , a.k.a. yellow death.

Wayne (though I very rarely call him by his first name) always wears his overcoat and sunglasses, no matter how sunny, cloudy, muggy, or cold the weather is. He looks like he's with the FBI, and he undoubtedly relishes the opportunity to envision himself an agent and not an elder. He cuts his own hair every ten days with a Kmart home barber kit on the quarter inch setting, which seems useless to me because his hair is invisibly thin and Scandinavian blonde anyway. Wayne was once tall enough to dunk a basketball. Now, forty pounds worth of peanut butter and jelly later, you can't fit a quarter-pound hamburger patty under his gym shoes when he jumps up in the air. He jokes about having bulked up, but with his newly acquired hips, we also joke about him having more of a girlish figure.

Parsons lifts up his recently purchased, five-dollar, 7-Eleven sunglasses and stares at me with iceberg blue eyes, as if he reads my mind, then bursts out, "Dude, d'ya get it?"

"Uh, yeah." I reply with sarcastic slowness. We keep on walking. We walk past Jacobs Field, the new Indians stadium, and continue our trek, my strides three quarters the length of my companion's. The joke Parsons told me was actually pretty funny—well not funny, but true. We are on the east side of town now. Supposedly Ice-T filmed a few videos here. Arsenio

Hall was raised in one of these neighborhoods. We walk by rows of government-subsidized housing projects. By the road, there is a huge billboard for Soul Glow hair products, and suddenly all of the other familiar advertisements are filled with differently pigmented individuals. Parsons, forever a Star Wars junkie, always calls this part of town the "dark side." Kentucky Fried Chicken. Colt .45. Sprite. Salem. Not only are all of the people in the ads black, but everyone on the street has changed color too.

We kick our way through broken malt liquor bottles and McDonald's wrappers to East 12th Street. "Hey faggots!" yells a kid from a passing low-rider Monte Carlo. The rattling trunk is attempting to cover some fourteen inch woofers that buzz to a smooth rapper's rhythm. With a chuckle, the kid pulls his Afro-with-pick-stuck-in hairdo back into the rusty car. Parsons and I both pretend we didn't hear anything.

"Jeez, dude, it never feels this hot in Idaho. It is hotter than heck. Let's hurry and get outta here," Parsons murmurs in Boisean protest. Our job for the afternoon is to deliver a video on how to make "better families" to a woman who is apparently interested in improving her own. Or, of course, she might just want a free, re-recordable videotape that is coincidentally the exact same length as an episode of The Simpsons.

The address of the house we are looking for is less than a block away now, so I offer to buy Parsons a Coke on the way home if he'll stop whining. (Not that I am the macho martyr type who loves pain and suffering, but we are ninety percent finished with an easy delivery.)

Then I notice something—two sketchy looking characters exiting a bar across the street and staggering over to the sidewalk directly in front of us. One guy is short, wiry, and greasy looking, with nickel-sized gaps between his front teeth. His partner is about Parsons's height, wearing sunglasses and a leather biker vest. The motorcycle guy looks meaner; the smaller fellow simply looks drunker. Neither one looks very good.

They are getting closer. I also observe something Parsons must be checking out as well. The small guy is wearing a few rings on his right hand. This wouldn't be a big deal, but my companion had just removed the butterfly bandage from his cheek, and his eye just recently un-blackened from when, a few weeks ago, he and another missionary were jumped by four guys who wanted their mountain bikes. The other Elder ran away, but Parsons "took a lickin' for the Lord," as he so eloquently put it. It amazes me that Parsons was beaten up. My companion has fists the size of milk jugs, and he was raised fighting every other weekend night at a dance or rodeo. He could have thumped the guys that tried to steal his bike, but he just stood there and endured the beating until some karate teacher ran out of his house and chased the hoodlums away. Parsons told me he had humbled himself like a biblical Paul, but the next time he was going to unload—or cut off some arms, which was more his style, like a Mormoniacal Ammon.

The two drunks are mumbling to each other in Jack Danielese about twenty feet in front of us when I notice that we are only two houses away from the safety of our appointment. We aren't quite close enough to run. "Hey you f—— rich boys," yells Greasy Guy. Ironically, neither of us is very wealthy. In fact we aren't planning on getting a paycheck for two years. But our standard summer uniform of slacks, pressed white shirt, tie, and black nametag doesn't exactly blend well in these inner city areas.

"Them's some nice clothes you got," crows Biker Man.

"What in the hell you doing down here by the projects?" chimes in Grease Guy. We are all wondering that exact same thing.

"We're missionaries," Parsons speaks "And we're coming to visit a lady in this house."

"Oh, they is f—— missionaries. Ya'll look like cops or f—— FBI to me," Grease Guy announces.

If Parsons hits this guy, then I better jump on Biker and try to hold him until the police come, I think to myself—that is, if the police even patrol this area. I know that my friend isn't going down without some action with his milk jugs. The drunks seem to be getting meaner.

"Well then, missionaries, we need a f—— ride to East 98th," grunts Biker Man.

"We don't have a car. We're walking," Parsons comments.

"Rich f—— like you, who got ties, ain't set up with wheels? F——
that," screams Grease with bloodshot eyes bulging and getting more hostile.

"Sorry, but we don't have a car," I cough. Biker Man reaches in his
pants and pulls out a .38 pistol and points it between my eyes (I know this
number only because Parsons tells me later). He laughs and waves the gun
around to show everyone that he is the boss.

"Give us a f—— ride man."

I don't know what to do. Who does in a situation like this? Maybe
Bruce Lee or Chuck Norris, but not me. I wonder if Parson feels the same
way. Then time actually does seem to be moving in a super kung fu theater
slow motion, and for no explainable reason, I just sidestep the two guys and
the gun, and I walk past them. Parsons is right next to me, and we are both
squinting our eyes and waiting to feel the bullets. We keep walking right up
to the house of our appointment, where we knock on our way into the
house.

Somehow we make it in alive, with our prayer-filled hearts bullet-
free. Immediately we ask for a phone to call 9-1-1.

The woman laughs and says, "Good luck. The police won't come
down here unless you got an emergency, and even then it takes 'em two
hours. Or two days."

We peer out the window and see the two men walking down the
street, two blocks away—obviously they must be having a hearty chuckle at
our naïve expense. We sit down. The house smells like cornbread, smoked
neck bone, and collard greens. I can hear some soothing gospel music
seeping in from a back room. We sit in silence, fidgeting with our shoelaces
and trying to get a grip on what has just happened. The lady is very polite
and offers us some of her "soul food."

"This cornbread's so good, it's going to make your tongue slap
your brain," she creaks in a gravelly voice. She laughs freely, moaning
"Hallelujah" every other word, and praising God in between.

"It's so good to see young'uns doin' the Lord's errand." Her dark
eyes look wise, nearly hidden behind seventy-five years' worth of wrinkles.

Behind her on the wall, is a portrait of a black Jesus. He is handsome, even nailed to a cross, with hair like lamb's wool. I have seen the same picture a few times before—in fact, I've seen the same picture with a white Christ, too. Parsons apparently sees the drawing at the same time as I do.

"Do you really believe the Son of God is black?" says Parsons. "Well, sugar, that's the way I like to think of him. Everybody's got their own ideas. I got mine. But I don't really think he's black, though."

"You're right. . . ." starts Parsons.

The lady interrupts, "But I believe he ain't like ya'll, either. Ya'll is pink, like an uncooked chicken leg. He is pure white, like the sun at noon."

Parsons doesn't have much else to say. He has had a long day. I have too. We talk a little bit more about a few gospel things and hand over the video. It seems a weak exchange for the safety of her home—an insincere video of smiling actors pretending to be brothers, sisters, and mothers, with no idea of how to keep a family together next to the projects on the East Side. I feel grateful. I feel out of place. I feel awkward and unsure, as I have during most of my time in Cleveland. I learn more lessons on these streets than I teach—and teaching is supposedly the reason that I am here.

As we leave, the lady gives us each a cold 7-Up for the long walk home, and she thanks us for the visit. As we close her door, she says something I'll never forget and probably never completely comprehend.

"Remember boys, it don't matter much about your color—you be who you be."

The drunks are long gone by now, to another seedy bar, praise the Lord. In silence, we walk back home through the broken bottles and the car exhaust, across the longest bridge in the world.

A GAY KIDNEY

I don't know if it is possible to have a gay kidney, but if it is, then Maggie Wong has one. She hasn't had it her whole life, but she wouldn't be alive now without it. I don't know—does a gay kidney function more flamboyantly or have better grooming habits and fashion sense than a non-gay one? Does it choose to be gay or is it born that way? I suppose it doesn't really matter, as long as it does the job, like clean your blood, right?

Maggie got the kidney from CJ when hers stopped working. He basically saved her life. The crazy thing is that he isn't even related to her. She has some weird blood type or something, so her parents couldn't donate, and she doesn't have any brothers or sisters. She was just lucky CJ was a match. It's weirdly amazing, when you think of it. If you're lucky, a nice home teacher might bring a plate of cookies or help to rake up your leaves. CJ was the Wong's home teacher and he gave Maggie one of his kidneys.

Maggie and I have been friends for a long time. We met in Sunday school class when I first moved to the Bay Area. We were the only non-blondes in the group of eight girls—the Mexican and the Asian. We cliqued right away and were tent mates at girl's camp that first summer. That was the summer we first met CJ, too.

He made the best mountain breakfast I've ever tasted on a camp stove—the pancakes weren't burned at all and the bacon was flat and crisp, but not burned and not too greasy. He organized all of the food for the trip, and he would have the menus of each meal written up in a color-coded calendar posted on the picnic table next to the wooden kitchen box. CJ wasn't married, but he was best friends with everyone in the Jensen family. He hung out at their house all of the time and drove to church with them every Sunday. In fact, it was Brenda Jensen who convinced him to get baptized and come and help with girl's camp. He had been visiting the church for a long time with them and I think most people just figured he was always a Mormon. He finally took the plunge.

Maggie and I grew close during those summers in the Sierras. Neither of us had much experience camping, so we could complain together about how dirty our hair got and how bad the latrine smelled. At the time the camp was a challenge and a chore, but as I look back twenty years later all I remember is how fun and carefree our summers were. You couldn't force me to sleep in a tent on the ground now, even if you offered me a thousand dollars. No way. Though it would be nice to get away from my kids for a night.

We went off to BYU and eventually came back to the same ward with husbands and babies. We were fatter and a bit greyer, but we remained friends and went to church together, often sitting in the foyer because we were late. We'd entertain our kids with dry Cheerios in Tupperware and pass notes back and forth when the High Council speaker was lulling everyone into a Sabbath coma. CJ was there during those years, sitting with the Jensens and giving Maggie and me a little wink when we walked in late. It was later that year that Maggie's health quickly declined and CJ stepped in to donate part of himself to save her.

Maggie improved remarkably well with some time and with the new kidney. She was back to her old stubborn self and would meet me at Ross when there was a forty percent off sale going on. It was actually at one of those sales that we ran into Brenda Jensen in her hour of distress and learned about the terrible news. We were shuffling through the shoe section to find size seven walking shoes for Maggie, and Brenda was shopping her blues away, pushing around a cart full of discounted jeans.

"Did you guys hear about CJ?" She asked with eyes looking red and hollow.

"No. What happened? Is he hurt?" Maggie responded.

"He's gone. He finally came out." Brenda said.

"Like came out, came out?" I questioned. "Like, out of the

closet?"

Brenda looked down. "Yeah. He moved in with his boyfriend in the city."

"Wow." Maggie continued.

"Wow," I added. We heard the elevator music in the background at Ross for the first time since we entered in the ensuing silence.

"Of course we all had inklings," we all nodded. Maggie continued, "not many men know anything about skin care products—and CJ could write magazine articles about taking care of yourself. But we all agreed—metrosexual right? Come on guys. We discussed this. He is a modern urban man and in touch with his feminine side."

"After all of these years. How long have you known him, Brenda? Forever right?"

"Yeah. Almost twenty years." She looked haggard. "Of course we always had suspicions. He actually talked to me about his issues a few times. I knew he was working on it. He had attractions and inclinations, but I thought he had it under control. He knew that God gives all of us challenges. He said he had made his choice. The gospel was more important to him."

"I guess he changed his mind." Maggie was not blessed with the art of tact.

Brenda began sniffling again. "He's probably been sneaking into the city to visit this guy for a long time. I don't know. I just don't understand. He could have talked to us."

"That kind of stuff happens," Maggie spoke up. "I heard there was a bishop over in the Concord Third Ward that was having an affair with his secretary for three years before he finally got caught. Secret lives."

"That is terrible," I couldn't help feeling angry and sad for anyone who treads water in a sea of lies for so long. And all of the family and friends involved. "Can you imagine?"

"Life. It happens," Maggie repeated.

"The new lifestyle these days demands freedom to do whatever you feel like. What happened to self-control? What happened to following the commandments? God doesn't give us any situation in life we can't handle. And the gospel doesn't change." Brenda was getting flustered. "Seriously, you guys. People today are so flaky—I love this cappuccino or wine or secretary and I don't care about what God wants. Forget commandments. Invent your own morality. Focus on Jesus's love and not the tables he turned over in front of the temple. *I need my freedom. I have to be me.* Like the Prop 8 stuff." She paused. "It's just not right. You have to be committed. We make promises. It is that simple."

"I know. It's hard, but we make covenants and need to keep them," Maggie added. "How do people live with themselves? Can they just rationalize every sin away? It starts small, but gets bad really fast."

"I'm sure it's not easy either way," I responded.

"What are you saying?" Brenda asked.

"I mean, imagine living with yourself if you were trying to live two lives or felt like you were not sure who you were? What if you felt that you were born that way?" I spoke up. "It can't be easy. It's hard for everyone involved, it must be terrible to live without integrity."

"If it's not easy then just don't do it," Maggie added. "The lines are clear. Hold to the iron rod. Straight is the gate and narrow is the way. It's not 'do what you want and it will be OK.' You can't form the rules around you to fit what you want from life. God doesn't change like that, no matter what Pop music or athletes say."

There was a lingering pause.

"I don't know. I think it is more complicated," I finally said.

"Only if you make it," Maggie replied.

A week later we all decided to meet for lunch at a Greens and

Things. It was a foggy day with a cold breeze rolling in from the coast. The restaurant always had great salads, but their soup choices were tasty and it was definitely a soup day. I got to the place before the others and found a table near the windows and sat down. After a few minutes I could see them walking in together and I was excited to chat. We talked about news and running the kids to soccer, but eventually the topic turned back to church.

"Well this brings us to the activity on Saturday ladies," Brenda announced. "You heard the bishop announce the meeting at the park and handing out flyers. I thought I'd bring the kids and make it a family project. We're making posters at home for the Prop 8 rally," Brenda announced. "Do you want to meet up?"

"What?" both Maggie and I exclaimed. "What are you talking about?"

We'd both heard a lot about Prop 8 and standing up for the democratic process of the majority of the people supporting something. We'd heard it spoken about in church. We'd heard of people donating money to support it—defending traditional marriage. Protecting the sanctity of the family. We'd heard of the General Authorities encouraging us to participate and be active in political activities. But Maggie and I must have been talking in the foyer when the announcement was made for a ward rally—we'd missed the news entirely.

"The bishop really announced for the ward to go the rally?" Maggie asked.

"Yes," Brenda replied. "We're all encouraged to go and let our voices be heard.

The Relief Society is bringing refreshments and the Elders' have been arranging different maps of the neighborhoods for families to divide up and go door to door.

"I don't think I can go," I whispered to Maggie. "I can't do it." I turned and spoke to Brenda, "I'm not sure I want to go." She looked puzzled and I continued, "This just doesn't sit right with me. It doesn't feel right. I love my family, but I don't think I can tell other people what their family should look like."

I looked toward Maggie for support. She glanced back nervously without blinking. The silence was momentarily broken when the server stopped by the table with a smiley, "Hello ladies! Can I take your order or get you drinks?"

She looked at each of us quickly and picked up on the uncomfortable body language and silence enough to reply, "Or maybe I'll give you just a few more minutes to discuss?" She backpedalled toward the kitchen.

"Maggie," I asked, "Don't you feel weird protesting against people like CJ? What if he wants to get married?"

"We can't always be silent," Maggie replied. "It's been made clear by the Brethren that we should let our voices be heard politically. He can get married to a woman. Keep working on his vice."

"Come on, that just doesn't work. It seems cruel and senseless," I replied.

"Honestly, you sounding pretty lukewarm. What is the scripture? Something about not hot nor cold and I will spew thee out," said Brenda. "What are you thinking?"

"I am thinking I should let my voice be heard. You said we are encouraged to speak up. I don't know about any *spewing*, but my voice doesn't like being told to protest and rally about something I'm not too sure about, and frankly, don't really agree with," I said.

"This may not affect you directly right now, Alejandra, but someday your religious rights will be taken away. Mark my words. If you don't take a stand, it may be too late," Brenda spoke up again. "The gay agenda will start us down the slippery slope that will end in anyone or anything that believes in traditional marriage being sued. Or forced to marry gays in the temple."

The server reemerged from the kitchen, took three steps toward our table, and turned the other way to speak with another table of customers on the other side of the restaurant.

"I just keep thinking about CJ," I said more quietly.

"Yeah, me too," answered Maggie.

"But CJ wouldn't vote for gay marriage guys. He knows what is right and wrong."

"It's true," Maggie said.

"Yeah, but I think he should be able to decide who he wants to marry for himself. It's his life and his voice. Let him decide. CJ getting married to his boyfriend doesn't hurt my own marriage." I replied. "I don't even care if he wants to go to the temple, though I highly doubt he would now."

"But in the future this could change your kids lives—and this could ruin kids now if they have two gay parents," Maggie said as she looked toward Brenda, who looked back with reassurance.

I couldn't take it anymore. I couldn't get CJ's face out of my mind. My feelings began to rise.

"Maggie—you have a gay kidney and it hasn't ruined you. CJ gave you your life back. I know he's not perfect, but I think he deserves to be happy as much as anyone." I looked at them both, took a deep breath, and stood up from the table. "I'm sorry, but I can't go to the rally. You are right about having a voice in politics and taking a stand. My voice is speaking now for me. Let CJ's voice stand for him. I am not going to the rally and if I am spewed out into the Telestial Kingdom or outer darkness, then so be it."

I walked out just as the server made her third attempt at approaching our table. I walked by her briskly and proceeded straight to my car with the rain sprinkling down my head and shoulders. I fiddled with the lock button for a few seconds and finally got in and sat down, sniffling. I couldn't tell which drops were rain and which were tears, but I wiped them off of my face and looked in the rear view to see my mascara running. I turned the key and shifted into gear. My hands shivered a little bit as I held the steering wheel tightly, and a faint beam of light broke through the clouds for a moment. I looked up just in time to see a slight rainbow over the Greens and Things sign. Within a few seconds the colors had faded and disappeared, but I felt a calming warmth rising from inside my chest as I drove back home in silence through the drizzling rain.

ABOUT THE AUTHOR

Alex Peterson lives in Utah with his wife Monica and two boys, Mateo and Elijah. He likes to hang out with them. He still likes to travel and often drags his family along. Most recently they lived for half a year in Santiago, Chile. His story, *Crossing the Bridge,* was a 2000 Brookie & D. K. Brown Fiction Contest Moonstone Winner and published in Sunstone Magazine. This collection of short stories was published so his kids could someday read them before they were thrown away or lost on a hard drive. He also writes music and plays guitar. If you like these stories check out his albums, Big Suckin Moose, Mexican Dog, and Pop a Wheelie on ITunes.